Staffords
Please re⁴

20

24

12

18

05

C000174148

3 8014 08299 6262

Stone Cold

By the same author

Stitched
Deceived

Stone Cold

Peter Taylor

ROBERT HALE · LONDON

© Peter Taylor 2010
First published in Great Britain 2010

ISBN 978-0-7090-9164-6

Robert Hale Limited
Clerkenwell House
Clerkenwell Green
London EC1R 0HT

www.halebooks.com

The right of Peter Taylor to be identified as
author of this work has been asserted by him
in accordance with the Copyright, Designs and
Patents Act 1988

2 4 6 8 10 9 7 5 3 1

Every word for my father and courageous mother
Ne Oublie – Never Forget
(Graham Clan motto).

Typeset in 11½/16pt Palatino
by Derek Doyle & Associates, Shaw Heath
Printed in Great Britain by the MPG Books Group, Bodmin and King's Lynn

Old Fred Torrance stared into his whisky as though he could see his whole past floating there in the liquid. Sitting opposite him, Frank, his elder son, slid his eyes in his father's direction, tried to gauge how much effect the drink was having. He didn't want to restrain him, but neither did he want him so far gone that he couldn't communicate with a modicum of sense.

The pub, in the town of Appleby, Cumbria, was bursting its buttons and most of the clientele were gypsies in town for the annual horse fair. Animated conversations cross fertilized so that standing back from the hubbub all anyone could have heard was a cacophonous jumble of nonsense, like feeding time in a menagerie.

Frank's gaze cut through the tables and the idle talk to one group of gypsies, the Jacksons, whose serious demeanour set them apart, as though they were stragglers from a funeral party who'd wandered in here by mistake. Frank shifted uncomfortably in his seat aware that they were watching him and his father like hawks watching prey. He knew that soon they would be crossing the room to join them and he didn't relish the prospect.

'He's out next week,' the old man suddenly mumbled into his glass, seeming to address, not his son, but a presence rising out of the whisky, from his wistful stare maybe an imaginary genie he hoped could grant him three wishes.

Frank arched an eyebrow. 'That's what I heard.'

'Won't be the same, your little brother,' the old man said. His eyes met his son's. 'Do you think he'll come back to us?'

Frank heard the emotion in his voice and studied his father. He didn't look well at all, not like the strong man who'd been a bare-knuckle fighter in his youth. Age and physical decline had mellowed him but occasionally in the eyes a spark still leapt up from the flint in his soul, hinting at the man he had once been.

'Five years,' Frank said. 'It's a long time.'

Old Fred returned his eyes to the glass, swirled it in his hand making miniature waves.

'We should have visited him.'

Frank sighed. This was old ground, miles behind them. Who could have guessed the old fool would turn sentimental about any of his family?

'What good would it have done? It would only have reminded him of what he was missing.'

'Never wrote to him,' the old man said plaintively. 'Can't write, can I? Missed him though.'

'He can't read or write either,' Frank said, the faintest of smiles playing on his lips. 'So what would have been the point?'

Frank watched the old man take another slug from the glass. He hoped the men across the room would make a move soon. His father had had enough and he didn't want to buy him another drink because it might just tip him too far.

'Five years!' Fred sighed. 'It's a lifetime when you're old.'

Frank frowned. His father really was overdoing the sentimentality. Where had it been hiding when he was young?

At the other side of the room the three Jacksons started to rise. Frank was glad things were starting to move. He was tiring of his old man's reverie. His new-found sensibility was sickening. For five years he'd managed fine with only an occasional bout of guilt about not visiting his son in prison. Was it just the drink making him maudlin? Had it reached into some far corner of his soul and disturbed part of him that he had never allowed expression before?

The Jacksons were weaving their way through the tables now. Those who recognized them became suddenly mute, shifted their chairs to clear a path for them. When they reached the Torrances' table, they formed a semi-circle. It was not hard to see one was the father, the other two the sons. Apart from the father's steel grey hair, they were all alike, burly, big-shouldered fellows whose facial features seemed to crowd too close together as though in competition for space. It gave them a mean look, pug ugly enough to give peas in the pod a bad reputation. As well as the grey hair, a broken nose distinguished Danny, the father. Both sons, Terry and Jet, as though neither wanted to be outdone by the other in the ugliness stakes, sported a cauliflower ear.

Old Fred Torrance lifted his head and looked at them. The light from the window fell across his face and Frank could see his eyes were watery and vague, knew the booze had settled in him like an old friend in a much-frequented home. Frank tried to remain optimistic. Fred could be mean when he was steeped in it and he had to hope he hadn't reached his fight-the-world stage.

'All right, Fred. All right, Frank.' The elder Jackson nodded to each in turn as he spoke.

'Mint,' Frank replied, and made a sweeping gesture with his arm. 'Take a seat, boys. It's been a long time since we sat down together, ain't it, Father?'

Fred said nothing. The scowl on his face said it for him as the Jacksons accepted Frank's invitation and swamped the free chairs with their considerable bulk. Frank watched his father throw down the last of his whisky. From the distasteful look on his face, it could have been foul-tasting medicine. Frank could feel a tug of war in his stomach. The Torrance and Jackson families weren't bosom friends. There was a history of bare-knuckle fighting on both sides and both sides had produced champions. The death of Bull Jackson, the elder Jacksons' younger brother, was the reason Henry Torrance had been sent to prison on a charge of manslaughter. Bull had been a famous champion, Henry Torrance a relative novice when they'd fought. His death from the blows he received in that fight was a scar on the Jacksons' pride. Rightly or wrongly, it had given Henry a certain twisted kudos amongst the crazier members of the fight brigade.

As an uncomfortable silence fell on the group, Frank and the two brothers exchanged meaningful glances.

'We hear your boy's getting out, Fred.' Danny's voice was halfway to a sneer.

Fred narrowed his eyes, gazed at him. Frank cast his

eyes downward, rubbed his jaw wondering whether his father would control himself, hoped he would.

'That's right,' Fred said, his voice clipped. 'He's getting out.'

'We hear he's been keeping fit,' Terry said. 'Using them fancy gyms they've got in prison.'

Fred's eyelids fluttered like birds' wings, closed, then as he turned to Terry ascended lazily.

'You know more than me,' he growled. 'How is that?'

Terry examined his fingernails as though he was bored. 'We've friends inside. We've kept tabs on him.'

Fred leaned back in his chair, eyed each of the Jacksons in turn.

'And what business is it of yours watching my boy? He's nothing to you. Five years he's been in that dump and he weren't going nowhere. He'd need wings, wouldn't he, and he weren't no angel.'

The words came out coherently, just a hint of a slur. Frank was glad that his father was far gone enough to be stirred, but not punchy and prepared to defy the odds against him, as he might once have done. It was how he wanted him.

Daniel Jackson sat forward, his shovel hands on his thighs, shoulders hunching forward like thick wings.

'That night Bull died,' he rasped, 'it was a fluke, a million-to-one chance, but it gave your boy a reputation he didn't deserve. They don't just say Henry Torrance who maybe would have beat Bull Jackson: they say Henry Torrance who killed Bull Jackson and they say it with awe, like he's a legend or something.'

'It's disrespectful,' Jet said, speaking for the first time, as though he'd been waiting for the malice he injected into the words to properly ferment before he let them out.

Perplexity wrinkled Fred's brow. His cheeks, already flushed with booze, took on a deeper hue. He looked at his son who avoided his gaze, so he turned it back on the Jacksons.

'Henry was a good fighter,' he said. 'That night was bad luck all round.'

Terry laughed scornfully. 'Good maybe, but there was only one Bull Jackson. Henry couldn't tie his laces.'

Fred couldn't help himself. They'd found his soft underbelly and he reacted.

'There's champions in our family. As many as in yours.'

Terry pulled at his cauliflower ear, somehow made the gesture impertinent. He glanced at Frank.

'Like Frank here you mean?'

All three Jacksons turned towards Frank with knowing grins. Frank lowered his head. He'd tried the fight game and he just didn't have it. Whatever it was in the Torrance blood that made them fighters had given him a wide berth. There was nothing to say.

'Chip Jackson, our cousin, he's the man now, the next King of the Gypsies,' Jet said.

Fred shrugged. 'Who's arguing, son?'

'But they still talk about Henry Torrance and in the same breath as Chip,' Daniel said, shaking his head, emphasizing his disbelief.

A small grin flirted on old Fred's lips. 'So what?' he hiccupped. 'What if they do?'

'He wasn't in the same class,' Daniel snapped, shoulders twitching. 'It's like comparing a racehorse with a workhorse.'

Bridling at the insult, Fred started to push himself out of the chair looking as though he was prepared to stuff Daniel's words back down his throat. Frank reached across, pushed him back down. Red-faced, struggling with his pride, he slumped back and Frank knew Danny was pushing all the right buttons, just hoped not hard enough to send him right into orbit.

'You were a champion – once,' Daniel sneered. 'Now you're just an old man and the acorns fell a long way from the tree.'

'Is that why you booze, Fred?' Terry followed up. 'Because you can't live your glory days through your sons?'

Jet grunted, 'It's pathetic.'

A bush fire ignited the old man's cheeks. Above the blaze, the wide barrels of his eyes fired volleys. Frank could see his father's frustration lay in the knowledge that, if he directed his rage physically, he would make a fool of himself, of what he had once been. Eventually he turned to Frank, his eyes appealing for his son to do or say something that would stop these puffed up Jacksons from besmirching the family name. But Frank just sat there saying nothing and the fire in him, like a guttering candle gradually surrendering its light, died away.

Seizing the moment, Daniel pressed on. 'Maybe we could settle it. Maybe Chip would fight Henry.' He winked at his sons. 'There again, there's a whisper Henry's gone soft in jail, and there's the prize money; I doubt anyone would sponsor him. You couldn't afford it, could you, Fred?'

Frank, his nerves on edge, watched his father's face,

wondering how he would react to yet another insult. Drink and rage had been a potent concoction in the old man's life, sometimes together, sometimes apart. He could see the old belligerence in the set of the jaw, the way his bottom lip protruded. Frank knew that in his day his father would already have kicked off. But time had taken its toll. The body that had once been so strong was too weak now, its still considerable bulk belying that illness had reduced its strength to not much more than a ten-year-old's. Breathing heavily, he rapped out words that once would have been punches.

'Our Henry will fight anyone. He's a Torrance. Could have been a champion if—'

The three Jacksons exchanged glances. Frank saw a gleam of triumph in their eyes as though they'd felt the tug on the line, knew all they had to do was reel old Fred in.

'Life's one big *if*, ain't it?' Daniel said, raising his eyebrows dismissively. 'And, like we say, we've heard Henry's gone soft. Got religion or something. Waste of time setting up a fight with him.'

Fred's big hands clenched into fists, the knuckles like snow-capped peaks.

'He ain't gone soft,' he spluttered, spittle issuing from his mouth. 'He'll show you. All I have to do is ask him.'

Daniel rubbed his jaw as though he was pondering the matter. He shook his head.

'Naw! You'd have to put up forty thousand minimum to fight Chip. You couldn't afford that even if you could persuade him. Best to let the Torrance name slide into obscurity.'

A slight quiver in his hand, Fred reached out for the

glass, picked it up, slammed it down again when he realized it was empty. He looked at his empty palm as though he was trying to read the future scored in the lines there. Suddenly, he held it out across the table, dangled it in front of the Jacksons.

Danny made no move to grasp it. 'You sure, Fred? You got forty thousand to give away, have you?'

Fred waved his arm impatiently. 'Man offers you his hand, you take it, no question.' He paused, stifled a burp. 'That's how it was in the old days.'

With a grin, Danny reached out and took the hand offered him. 'All right, Fred,' he said as they shook. 'We've sealed it and there's no going back.' He held onto the old man's hand and bellowed out above the noise in the room.

'Everybody see this! Chip Jackson will fight Henry Torrance. Each fighter puts in forty thousand and the winner takes all.'

There was a second's silence, then a flash went off, followed by others as those in the room who had cameras took pictures. Then, gradually, the noise rose, reached an even higher pitch than before as the latest bit of news to hit Appleby fair reverberated around the room. Danny let go of Fred's hand. The old man, startled by the flashes, had a bemused look, like a stage-struck actor frozen in the footlights on his first night.

Danny stood up, followed by his sons. Self-satisfaction dripped off them like grease from fried bacon. Fred stared at them as though through a curtain of mist, as if the whisky he'd consumed had finally numbed his senses and he'd retreated into an alternative world only he was aware of.

'Let's hope he loves you enough to fight,' Danny said. 'You've got forty thousand reasons to hope so.'

As they swaggered their way back to their table, Jet turned and said, 'Have a nice day, Fred. Got to make the most of them at your age.'

Frank watched them go and said nothing. His father maintained that self-hypnotic stare, while the silence between them stretched into an arid desert that seemed to have no prospect of an horizon, until Frank finally gave it one.

'Satisfied, are you?'

Fred's eyes swivelled, locked onto his son's. The lost look vanished, was replaced by bitter disappointment that turned to accusation. Frank averted his own eyes.

'Where were you?' Fred said. 'Where were you?'

Frank bridled, snapped his eyes back to his father. 'Watching you flush forty thousand down the pan. That's where I was.'

'Henry would have stood up to them,' Fred said, his voice forlorn. 'Them and their big mouths.'

Frank snorted, 'He'll have the chance now, won't he? If you can persuade him to fight, that is.'

'He'll do it for me – when he knows about this.'

'Let's hope he'll still take notice of you,' Frank grunted. 'Let's hope he even wants to know you.'

Doubt clouded the old man's face, found its way into his eyes, took root there. He knew he had risked just about all his savings. Lowering his head, he mumbled in a voice denuded of all pride, 'You'll have to help me persuade him, Frank.'

'Don't worry,' Frank told him. 'A man coming out of

prison needs money. The question is whether he's prepared to take a beating – whether he still has the nerve.'

The old man rubbed his face with his hand as though the action could remove the foolishness of the last few minutes. Frank didn't have any pity because he didn't consider he'd been enough of a father to deserve it and he didn't let pity rule his emotions anyway.

'Between us we might just persuade Henry,' he continued. 'Can't have all that money running away down the road, can we?'

Fred gave him a sideways glance. 'Half it will be yours one day. You've got a vested interest here.'

Frank nodded. He knew that little fact too well. 'Let's get out of here,' he said, 'before you spend it on booze.'

He guided his father to a door keeping well away from the Jacksons' table. Just before he exited, he glanced back across the room in their direction. They were watching him with identical grins as though they'd been choreographed. In return, Frank gave a slight nod of his head.

Seated on his hard bed, Henry Torrance glanced up at the bars of his cell. Familiar prison sounds drifted to his ears, sounds which had at first been alien and disturbing but now, after five years, were no more than an occasional irritant, even at times strangely comforting in their familiarity. He was aware routine had been his saviour but soon that routine would be broken. Those sounds and prison smells would be no more, except perhaps in his dreams. In two days he would be released, penance served, society paid its dues. Bubbles of perspiration burst onto his brow and his blood gave a sudden rush. For sure, he was ready for his freedom but he wondered whether he would cope. He was different from the callow youth who had entered these walls. The world outside would have changed too. Could the different man adapt to the different world without reverting to old habits?

He squared his muscular shoulders, looked down at the massive hands resting on his thighs. The hands triggered the memory, pulled him down the dark path he had trodden so many times. Those hands, what they were capable of, had brought him here. Yet hands were only an instrument. It was something inside him that had unleashed them, given them the power to beat another human being to death. Bull Jackson hadn't been much and he'd known the score, but no man should die like that. He remembered the pictures in the newspapers, Bull's wife and three children standing by his grave, heads bowed in a miserable black-and-white tableau which his madness, as if by God given right, had created. Why had his own family put him in that situation in the first place?

He placed a hand over his eyes as though to hide from a past best left undisturbed. It was the old gypsy life that had been responsible for leading him into the fateful fight. In prison, being forced to mix with others of different creeds, attending education classes, he'd learned things, gradually emerged from the cocoon of beliefs and prejudices his gypsy life had woven round him. The gypsy way, which had been his heritage, had a lot going for it, but he'd done with it now. There was a whole world out there and he was determined he was going to embrace it with an unshackled mind.

Henry heard a key turn in the lock, turned towards the

door as a screw let his pad mate in. Tom Daly, a gypsy like himself, slumped his emaciated frame down on his own bed and let out a sigh. Henry didn't like the agitated look in his eye, the aura of apathy about him. He was having trouble adjusting to prison, the way a wild bird has trouble adjusting to the confines of a cage and dies of a broken heart. Sometimes Henry caught him staring into space and it wasn't just down to the drugs; it was his broken spirit dreaming of horizons denied him here. You couldn't afford to dwell on such things if you wanted to remain sane.

'How'd the visit go, Tom?'

Tom shook his head. Eyes that seemed only half aware stared out from hollowed cheekbones. Henry saw the desperation in them.

'Bad news, man,' he groaned, focusing on a spot on the ceiling as though the words were addressed to some invisible presence. 'The wife has no more money, can't buy me the drugs and the Jacksons aren't going to give me any on tick.'

Hearing the Jackson family mentioned, Henry grimaced. Bull Jackson, the man he'd killed, had been their hero and talisman, the best of their fighting men following in a long line. If he'd killed him in any other way than in a prize fight, they'd have wreaked their vengeance upon him. They'd always been involved in a multiplicity of dodgy businesses but drug dealing was beyond the pale, a sin compounded when they dealt to their own kind.

'You could apply to go on the drug-free wing, Tom. You'd get counselling and they make sure there's no drugs around. They'd put you on methadone, wean you off the brown and the rest.'

17

Tom didn't answer, just nodded automatically, like a wound-up doll. He'd heard it all before, didn't really want to know. He swung his legs up on to the bed and lay on his back.

'I don't know what I'm going to do,' he said, a melancholy timbre in his voice. 'You've been here for me, Henry. Nobody else will be. It takes a gypsy to understand one. They'll likely pad me with an idiot or bully when you're gone and it'll drive me madder than I already am.'

A lonely wind trapped in the courtyard below the window sighed its frustration as it beat against the walls. Seagulls cried out as though in answer, their voices reminiscent of rolling seas stretching as far as the eye could see. Henry had already told Tom what he needed to do, didn't like to press it. Like all addicts, Tom had to want to do it for himself.

'Drug-free wing!' he repeated.

'I only feel free when I'm tripping, man,' Tom answered edgily.

Henry shut up. His hope was that, without him there to help when the highs wore off and he descended into depression, Tom would realize he'd have to seek help elsewhere, either sink deeper into murky waters, or start to kick to the surface.

Suddenly, Tom said,' Anyway, didn't know you planned to fight. You never told me.'

Henry's head jerked back. What was Tom talking about? Had the drugs affected his brain so that it was creating fictions from odd fragments of memory?

'You know I'll never fight again.'

Tom levered himself up onto his elbows, met Henry's gaze.

'Sorry, mate! It was the wife told me. She heard there's talk at Appleby. They're saying you'll fight the latest Jackson prospect. Big money involved too. That's what she said, anyway.'

Henry's eyebrows arched. Was his past beating a path to his door even before he was out of here? He battened down his anger. It was probably rumour. There was plenty of idle talk at Appleby Fair. He was aware that Tom was studying him, his stare calculating, knew he was thinking that if Henry fought and won he'd have money, might help him by sending in some of what he craved.

'Forget it,' he snapped. 'It's just somebody making mischief. The horses at Appleby have more sense than their owners. You know where you stand with horses.'

The glimmer of hope in Tom's eyes gave way to disconsolation as he saw another door closing in his face. Henry couldn't sustain his anger though. Tom was out of order even broaching the subject when he was aware why Henry was in here, but given his need, expecting him not to try would have been like expecting a drowning man to ignore a lifejacket.

Minutes later it was all forgotten and Tom was asleep. Down the corridor Henry heard footsteps, a screw's voice announcing it was time for a library visit. He picked two books off the shelf above his bed, flicked idly through the pages. It was still a wonder to him that he had learned to read. Books had opened up a new world for him, as though his mind had lain in hibernation for years, had at last emerged, like a hungry bear from its winter cave, to a landscape of infinite possibilities.

A key turned in the lock. The door opened and screw with a long, angular jaw poked his face into the cell.

'Take all your books back today, Torrance,' the screw announced. 'Dare say you'll never lift one on the out, eh! Once you get dodging and weaving again with all your gypsy mates.'

'Don't know about that, Mr Evans. Guess I'll always have my – chin – in a book.'

Once he would have let the screw's taunting get to him but it was the measure of the change in him that he could keep his cool, find other methods of retaliation. The screw wasn't sure whether or not he was being sent up. No matter what the screw thought, Henry knew he'd be reading, maybe even studying, on the out. Let the ignoramus have his pennyworth.

With other prisoners from the wing, he followed Evans through a labyrinth of corridors. They waited at each door while the screw laboriously opened up and then locked it behind them. Until recently, the library had been Henry's place of work and he'd become acquainted with the civilian librarians who worked there. One of them, Mary Thompson, had become another wonder in his life.

Evans let them into the library and Henry was pleased to see Mary at the desk. She glanced up, offered a smile, withdrew it when Evans looked in her direction.

The prisoners dispersed down the aisles wanting to make use of the ten minutes they were permitted to choose fresh books. Henry glanced idly at the non-fiction, plucked a book on horse care from the shelves, flipped through the pages but didn't absorb much of the content. It was a subject he was familiar with anyway, having worked with horses before.

'Let's roll,' the screw called out dead on the ten minutes. 'Too much knowledge is a bad thing for you lot. Never know what you'll do with it.'

They lined up at the desk to return the books they'd read and have new ones stamped. Henry positioned himself at the back watching Mary go about her business, admiring the way she treated each man in the same friendly manner.

'I'm losing a customer,' she said, when it was his turn. Her blue eyes twinkling, she tossed back her blonde hair. 'No doubt you'll be pursuing other interests soon, Mr Torrance.'

Henry smiled, glanced towards the door where Evans was preoccupied patting a prisoner down. He lowered his voice to a whisper.

'Part of me will be out there, but the best part of me will be wherever you are, Miss Thompson.'

She laughed as she picked up his books, then leaned forward, fixed him with her baby blues and whispered, 'Reassuring to know I'm not just another brick in the wall then.'

He was about to answer when Evans called out, 'Come on, Torrance. These bookworms are waiting for you and I'm ready for my bait.'

'Knowledge is the food of the mind, Mr Evans,' Henry called back, glancing disdainfully in his direction. 'You should maybe change your diet.'

One of the prisoners stepped up to be searched, diverting the screw's attention. Henry took his chance, placed his hand over Mary's. It was a rare moment of physical contact, the warm smoothness of her skin surprising him in a world where most of the time everything seemed rough, hard edged. It reminded him of how much he had missed. As a youth, he'd been one for the girls. Five years was a long time without a female's touch, or soft words to alleviate the asperity of prison conditions. In here, gentleness was weakness, an opening where those with a vicious temperament would drive home their weapons, either of the material or verbal variety, with glee.

Walking back through the corridors, he remembered how, like Tom Daly, the gypsy in his soul had once cried out at the restrictions. But some people had been kind to him, prisoners and screws, and life had become bearable. Eight months ago Mary had come into his life, like a light shining into the grey austerity. She had become the star in the corner of his universe. That she had returned his feelings, when he had summoned the courage to declare them, had seemed like a kind of miracle.

Back on the wing again, Henry called out to the screw, 'Want me to tell your fortune for you, Mr Evans? Learned the skill at my old grandmother's knee, I did.'

The prisoners laughed and Evans swung round, his jaw thrust forward so that it looked even more prominent.

'Got to cross your palm with silver, haven't, I Torrance? Wouldn't trust you with a five pence piece, would I?'

Henry grinned 'You've thwarted me again, Mr Evans. Thought you'd like to know what's in front of you and – I confess – I just wanted to hold your hand for the last time before we part for ever.'

A prisoner wolf whistled and the others smirked.

Blushing, Evans turned his head away, spoke to Henry over his shoulder.

'Don't count your chickens, Torrance,' he said, spitefully. 'For ever is a long time.'

'Used to steal chickens,' Henry came back at him, smiling. 'Never had time to count them though.'

The banter ended as the prisoners filtered into their own cells. Tom still lay on his bed but awake and looking more apathetic than ever. That worried Henry. It was natural enough to dwell on life outside for a while but there came a day when you had to let go, steal yourself to live in the present or you'd go mad. He'd seen it happen often enough.

Out of the blue, Tom said, 'Maybe I could learn to read and write like you did. I never worked much at school see. We was always moving on and it didn't seem to matter.'

'Best thing you could do,' Henry told him, hoping this was a new, positive note. 'Keep you out of mischief – and other things.'

He did his best to inject belief into his voice but could hear the false note. He didn't really think Tom was serious, was merely voicing a thought that flitted into his mind. A long road lay between thought and action when you were courting heroin. His thoughts returned to Mary Thompson. One hint of their relationship and he'd have been moved to another prison and Mary would have lost her job. Continuing their relationship on the out was equally dangerous for Mary because it would be regarded as a danger to prison security. What if all his good intentions came to nothing? It was all very well making plans. So many did that, but failed to escape their past, reverted to their old ways. He worried about failing himself and her. He hadn't much to offer and he didn't want Mary backing a loser. Best he got a foot on the ladder, started climbing before they made a final commitment to each other.

An hour later, Evans opened up the cell again and stepped inside. He put his hands together in an attitude of prayer and raised his eyes to the heavens.

Henry shot him a querulous look. 'What is it this time, Mr Evans? Conscience worrying you, is it? Come to make last-minute confession of all the wrongs you've done me?'

'Arise from your pit of iniquity, Torrance,' Evans intoned. 'God is calling you and I am a mere emissary.'

Henry knew Evans was referring to Father Andrew, the priest to the gypsy community on Teesside. This must be a last visit to wish him well for his release. He scowled at the screw. The father's kindness had been part of his survival here and he didn't like Evan's disrespectful words or tone.

For the second time that day Henry followed where Evans led. When they arrived at the prison chapel, the screw unlocked the door and stood back, ushering Henry in. Evans closed the door and remained outside. Father Andrew, his ruddy complexion contrasting to Henry's prison pallor and enhanced by the contrast to his shock of white hair, sat in a chair facing the door. Behind him was a small altar and cross. The priest smiled, beckoned him to a chair facing his own.

'I'm pleased you've asked to see me,' Henry said. 'I was hoping you would.'

Father Andrew smiled and ran his hand through his

hair. Henry felt again the aura of peace which seemed to accompany him and encompass those who were in his presence. He wished his own father had possessed just a fraction of it.

'I came to wish you luck,' the priest said. 'But there is that other motive, the one we have discussed.'

'You want me to be baptized?' Henry said.

'Only if you can fully accept.'

Henry looked into the placid blue depths of the priest's eyes, found no hint of pressure there, nor in his benign expression. He knew the least he owed this man was the truth, what was in his heart.

'Father, you've done a lot for me, you and your beliefs, for which I am eternally grateful.' He was conscious of Father Andrew watching him, a wise and patient knowingness swimming to the surface of those blue eyes as though he already knew what Henry was going to say.

'I'll never forget what I've learned from you, Father. And I do believe in the ways of Jesus.'

He hesitated and the priest said it for him. 'But you cannot accept the God of the Bible.'

Henry sighed. 'I killed a man, Father. Something evil came into me for a few moments, a desire to destroy a man utterly. You'd probably call it the Devil and you could be right. I won't be letting the Devil in again, but I don't understand how God can give him so much power to do harm.' He lowered his head. 'I can't be a hypocrite, Father.'

The priest nodded, reached out and patted his shoulder in a way that Henry wished his own father could have done.

'Maybe one day,' he said. 'You've travelled a long way

and sometimes the last mile, that leap of faith, is the hardest.' Father Andrew sat back. 'But enough of that. I've other news for you.'

Henry feigned a grimace. 'They've made a mistake with my release date. An error in the paperwork. That Devil at work again.'

'On the contrary, rather good news. I've visited your old trainer Mick Lane in South Bank. He'd like you to do some coaching with the youngsters at the community centre.'

'Me?' Henry gasped. 'Coach boxing?'

'To young lads, in an area that's full of temptations for them. It's needed, believe me.'

'But – after what I've done?' Henry couldn't keep the astonishment out of his voice.

The priest shrugged, as though it was a matter that didn't require much consideration.

'Proper boxing with rules, the way Michael taught you. Boxing that instils discipline in wild youngsters, saves many of them going down the wrong road.'

Henry shook his head, still disbelieving. 'And my probation officers have agreed to that?'

'No reason not to and, even better, Michael has contacts, thinks he might be able to get you a job that's right up your street. Not to be sniffed at, is it? There's not much going especially—'

'For ex-cons living in South Bank.'

'It's a fact of life, son, and there are, shall we say alternative lifestyles in South Bank. It's a tough area.'

The priest hesitated, his expression like a man's about to take a first, tentative step into a minefield. 'Your father is living permanently on the site there and your brother has a caravan on the site he often uses.'

Henry screwed his face up. 'You're talking about the dead now, Father. As you well know they never visited me, never made any contact.'

Father Andrew studied him with sad eyes. 'I pray one day you and your family might be reconciled.'

'There are better prayers, ones that might be answered.'

Father Andrew raised his hands in a gesture that said he knew when to back off. He was well aware Henry had been hurt so badly his negative feelings towards his family were almost set in concrete.

'You were lucky your aunt left you her house when she died,' he said, changing the subject. 'She must have thought a lot of you.'

Henry nodded. 'She was my mother's sister and I was the only one who bothered with her when my mother died. My father and brother didn't visit her. True to form, you might say.'

Father Andrew smiled sagely, as though at some secret knowledge he had in reserve.

'There's goodness in you, Henry Torrance,' he proclaimed, 'as there is in a lot of men I visit in prison. In very few men does the light ever dim entirely.'

'Comes pretty close in some, Father.'

As he spoke, Henry's eyes drifted over the priest's shoulder to the figure of Christ on the cross.

'I was going down some bad roads before Her Majesty opened her door to me,' he continued. 'Who knows where they might have led? This place has changed me.'

'One door closed and another opened. It's to your credit you made use of your opportunities.'

Henry looked down at his hands. His forehead puckering into worry lines, he muttered, 'And tomorrow I'll close another door behind me.' He brought his eyes back to the priest's. 'It scares me, you know – the road to Hell is paved with good intentions. Isn't that what they say?'

'It's only natural to be scared, son. Five years is a long time. Go to see Michael as soon as you're settled. Keeping busy is important.'

Henry smiled. 'I've a lot to thank you for.'

They rose together. Henry turned to the priest, an earnest look on his face. When he spoke again, he could hear his old guilt breaking through to the surface.

'What I did will always be with me.'

Father Andrew hesitated, trawled for his answer, gave it softly. 'How could it be otherwise?'

Henry shook his head. 'It's a terrible thing to take a man's life. There's so many ripples – his wife, his children, his grandchildren yet unborn. I've cursed them all.'

Father Andrew's face was full of concern. 'You have to live with it, Henry. Keep busy or you will mope. In good works lies your redemption. You have to hold on to that.'

'I'll try,' Henry said.

They walked to the door. Henry suddenly remembered his pad mate.

'I'm concerned about Tom Daly, Father. You know him, don't you?'

The priest thought for a minute. 'I know him a little. He's serving a one year sentence.'

'Yes, but the way he's going, I'm not sure he'll make it. I'm hoping you can help.'

Henry elaborated while the priest listened with growing

28

concern. He wouldn't have discussed the source of Tom's troubles with just anybody. But he knew Father Andrew wasn't naïve about drugs in prisons and would find a diplomatic way to help Tom. The screws knew what went on, of course, but there were those who connived at the drug taking because they believed it made for an easier life for them if a prisoner got what he craved.

'With his supply shut down, I'm not sure whether he'll flip,' Henry concluded. 'He's dependent and I've been trying to look after him but when I go. . . .'

The priest's lips drew back. Henry could see his teeth clenching. It gave him a feral look far removed from his normal, benign self.

'That insidious evil penetrates even these walls,' he groaned. His cheeks puffed out as though they were about to explode. 'Time they put a stop to it. Drugs, Henry, create monstrous waves.'

'You'll do what you can for him, Father?'

'Of course. And don't worry, I won't mention our conversation to anybody.'

They shook hands and Henry stepped out into the corridor where the screw was waiting for him.

'Confession time over?' Evans sneered as they started back to the wing. 'Who's fooling who. Leopards don't change their spots.'

Henry looked at him sideways. 'Learning my vows actually.'

'What?'

'It's what you do when you're going to be a priest.'

Evans went quiet, mulling that one over, not quite sure. Henry looked straight ahead, smiling inwardly.

As they entered the wing, Evans shook his head 'Naw! They wouldn't take you.'

'Equal opportunities, isn't it? Politically correct and all that,' Henry told him, his face deadpan. 'They're short of gypsies in the priesthood. Bit like when they recruit prison officers, I suppose. In your work they have to have a certain mix of those with brains and those with muscles. Did they tell you why they chose you, Mr Evans? If it was me, I'd be curious.'

The screw looked nonplussed. He was still trying to work that one out as he opened Henry's cell. Henry bowed his head to him just before he closed the door.

'Bless you, Mr Evans!' he said. 'Don't work those muscles too hard.'

It was the penultimate day before his release. Henry awakened as the sunlight squeezed its way through the bars making long shadows on the wall. He smiled at the thought of freedom being so close. These sparse surroundings would gradually fade into memory and the sun on his face would no longer be a sought after luxury. If he wanted, he'd be able to lie in it all day, catch up on what he'd missed. Freedom! At last, he dared to imagine it as more than a word.

He threw his legs off the bed and sat up. Opposite him, Tom had his eyes shut but didn't seem at rest. His shoulder muscles were twitching spasmodically like a dog's when it dreams. Henry wondered what torments were stalking his subconscious mind so that even asleep he wasn't resting properly.

He started his usual morning exercise regime. When he

was halfway through, a screw opened the door, called out that it was shower time. That woke Tom who pushed his scrawny frame off the bed and looked down at Henry who was performing sit-ups. Pulling a face, he flexed first his right arm muscle, then his left, affected a pained expression, as though he was feeling the strain.

'Right, Mr Universe,' he said. 'That's my exercise for the day. No one will kick sand in my face. Best go get a shower.'

Henry smiled up at him, pleased to see his sense of humour. This morning he seemed to have awakened in a more cheerful mood.

'Watch you don't slip down that plug hole,' he called out, laughing as Tom exited with his towel wrapped around him. 'It's a long swim to the North Sea, mate, and they'll think you've tried to escape.'

Henry finished his exercises, wrapped his towel around his waist, sauntered down the corridor towards the showers. He'd followed his routine long enough, tended to notice any little nuance that differentiated one day from any other. Almost subconsciously, his mind knew the latitudes it would allow without concerning itself. Survival could depend on noticing little things, a look, a movement. Right now, Henry registered that a few more men than usual at this time of morning were out on the landing, three of them men he didn't have time for. He considered them parasites, hangers-on always on the look out for fresh sensation so they could be the harbingers for better men, in the hope their tales would edge their status up a notch. They'd seen him come out of the cell and now their heads were bobbing. One of the screws, a weak man easily manipulated, normally positioned himself near the showers. This morning he was standing at the opposite end of the landing fidgeting with his key chain as though his life depended on him counting every link. He glanced up at Henry, dropped his eyes too quickly. A nagging ache started in Henry's stomach. He picked up his pace, hoping his instincts were wrong.

Mason, a brute with a thick neck, was leaning on the wall outside the showers, one arm stretched languidly across the entrance. Henry halted in front of him and glared. Mason blinked at him like a man shaking off a punch, didn't look as though he knew how to react. He was an inch shorter than Henry's six foot two but much heavier, though most of his bulk came from weight training. Henry had seen small men who were tigers in action, knew size could deceive you. Bulk for its own sake didn't impress him.

'Move!' he snapped, trying to keep cool and suppress a rage he could feel rising inside him.

'Stay out of it, Torrance,' Mason said, finding his voice. 'It's business.'

Henry knocked his arm out of the way and walked past him into the shower room. Clouds of steam partially obscured his vision, but he could see three naked bodies at the far end. One of those bodies, the scrawniest, belonged to Tom Daly. Two men in threatening poses were holding him against the wall. Henry swallowed. Why was this happening on this of all days?

He recognized the two men holding Tom as lower ranking hardcases. They knew his past reputation as a boxer and he hoped that might help him. Glancing over his shoulder, he saw that Mason had taken up a predatory stance a few yards behind him. Henry figured he was waiting to see which way the wind was going to blow before he made a move. Three against one were good odds for them. But he could do them a great deal of damage before he went down and they would know that.

'You're finished with him,' Henry said, as one of the men drew back his arm to strike Tom. 'Leave him be.'

The two men turned, mouths open. For a moment, they seemed frozen in time, like a video on pause. Henry waited, wondering which of the two would be the first to press play, let the future commence. Emerging unexpectedly like that from the swirling steam, he'd surprised them. That advantage needed pressing home quickly because it wouldn't last.

'You should be ashamed of yourselves,' he said, shifting his position slightly so he could keep an eye on Mason as well. 'Three of you against a lightweight.'

One of the men, bald and pudgy, stuck out his bottom lip. With his roly-poly body partially wrapped in a white towel, the action made him look even more like an overgrown baby in an oversized nappy.

'Stay out of this, Torrance,' he hissed. 'It's not your business. We're doing this for a Jackson. He owes fifty quid. You know the game.'

'Yeah!' his mate chimed in. This one was built like a high jumper, tall, skinny arms and legs. 'He's had time. You know how it works. You pay your debts or else.'

Henry faltered. Damn Tom for his foolishness! He'd known what the consequences would be if he broke the rules. There were plenty of examples. Not many in here would sympathize with him if he hadn't paid a debt. But he couldn't let these men have their way. Tom was far too weak to take the damage.

The tension stretched out, a taut rope in a tug of war, nobody willing to let it go. Like meddlesome ghosts, clouds of steam danced around them. Henry's body felt as though a furnace was burning inside it. If all hell broke loose, he wouldn't be walking out tomorrow. Even if he survived, they'd likely extend his sentence. But how could he avoid it? Through the steam his pad-mate's face loomed, eyes glazed, his stick thin body like a famine victim's. The sight of him renewed Henry's resolve. Walking away wasn't an option. If he did, he knew it would live with him the rest of his life.

As the time spun out, the men visibly grew in confidence. Henry could see the same thought passing between them. Was Torrance a busted flush, all talk? Had he walked into this thinking he was still the man, suddenly lost his bottle? Henry didn't want to fight but he'd have to do something soon. He decided to try for a compromise, praying they'd accept it.

'I'll pay you,' he said, adding in a menacing tone. 'Either that, or we get down to it.'

The baby spoke first. 'When will you pay?'

'I've got a stash. I'll send it round tonight.'

The men exchanged glances, weighing the odds. Torrance could do them damage before they put him down. No doubting that. Was it worth it when he was willing to give them what they wanted? Cash or carnage? No choice really. In their silence, there was mutual, unspoken agreement.

'We'll accept that,' Lanky said. He gave Tom a shove. 'Better than relying on this piece of nothing. He's had his lesson anyway.'

They stepped away from Tom, staring at him as though he was a creature that had crawled out of a rubbish tip. Henry moved forward, helped him up.

'You won't be here to help him next time, Torrance,' Baby sneered as they walked out.

Henry let out a breath. It had been a close thing. He felt anger towards Tom for bringing him to this. But had he the right to judge when he'd committed the ultimate sin himself?

Back in the cell they both lay on their beds. Tom had received the beginnings of a working over, not the full Monty and, a few bruises apart, was more shocked than anything. He's muttered his thanks to Henry a few times but Henry had been quiet, preoccupied with his own surfeit of emotion as he realized how close he'd come to jeopardizing his future.

Eventually, Tom turned his head towards Henry. Looking shamefaced, he shook his head. His voice was hoarse, like a wind cutting its way through dry reeds.

'God, Henry, I nearly blew it for you.'

Henry wanted to be angry but couldn't get off the mark, especially when he saw tears streaming down Tom's cheeks in genuine contrition. Besides, he was still contending with his own emotions. Today, in those showers, the rage inside him had resurrected itself. He hadn't allowed it scope for a long time and feared what it could do to him. His consolation was that today, anyway, he'd managed to hold it on a tight rein.

'You didn't tell me you owed the Jacksons.'

35

'I was ashamed. I'll pay you back, Henry – every penny.'

Henry didn't expect to see the money again, at least not for a long time, but he knew Tom meant what he had said.

'Be careful, Tom. That was a close thing.'

Tom whined, 'What'll I do when you're not here to protect me?'

Henry sighed his exasperation. 'You know what you should do,' he snapped. 'You just won't do it, will you?'

Tom stared at him. 'I remember those days on the road,' he said, wistfully, 'the green fields, the birds singing in the hedgerows, always moving on, nothing ever stale, every day different.'

'Those days are gone,' Henry said. 'Most gypsies prefer living on sites now. It had to happen in a modern world. We need to integrate, break down barriers.'

'I'll always be a gypsy,' Tom said, as though to himself. 'I'll always prefer the open road.'

Henry didn't answer. What could he say? He realized he might as well try to change the colour of Tom's skin, those Romany features imprinted on his face. His pad mate just couldn't grasp what he was talking about. Altering your life wasn't easy when there were generations of gypsies in your soul, when it was hard enough to live in a house, never mind the claustrophobia of a cell.

The rest of the day passed without incident. Tom was strangely quiet, which Henry figured must be due to the fact he was sore after his beating and not a little shocked.

Henry was reading a book when the lights went out. Even now, after all his time in prison, he couldn't get used to the way someone else decided when your day was to end, the suddenness of the plunge from light to darkness. It made him feel like an animal, his life controlled by a mad scientist conducting an experiment in sensory deprivation. He could remember how, as a boy and youth, he'd lived according to the sun's dictates, took that freedom for granted.

'Demons!' Tom suddenly yelled out. 'All around me!'

Henry turned his head to look at him, couldn't make out his face, only his shape on the bed. The demons frequently came to Tom at night, conjured from the black thoughts that can enter a man's mind in the darkness when there is nothing to distract him from his loneliness, when he gets to wondering what peculiar fate has decided he should live and die and what purpose does his existence serve anyway. Tom, under the influence of drugs, was becoming more paranoid by the day. Henry prayed Father Andrew would set wheels in motion to help him before it was too late.

'They won't get me, will they, Henry? You won't let them.'

'I won't let them, mate. You're safe.'

'That's all right, then,' Tom called back, his voice calmer. 'Cos they're horrible.'

Silence descended again. Unlike Tom, Henry found the darkness comforting, a place where he didn't have to be constantly watching out. He drifted off into a long, deep sleep and dreamed he was riding a gypsy horse through a field of yellow buttercups. The sky clouded over, thunder rolled across the heavens and, between flashes of lightning, he glimpsed a figure running ahead, was nearly sure it was

37

his pad mate. The horse rose on its hind legs in fright, tried to throw him. He woke perspiring. It had been so real and he wondered at the strange workings of the mind as he turned over onto his side to look across at Tom's bed.

There was just enough light from the moon for him to see the bed was empty. Where was Tom? He noticed a pair of trainers on the floor. They were upright, not lying flat. Surely those were ankles projecting from them. Suspicion spiralled through his brain. He threw back his duvet, sat bolt upright, compelled his eyes to travel where they didn't want to go, upward from those splayed feet.

His vision had made enough adjustment to make out Tom's staring eyes, the tongue bulging from his mouth in what seemed like a grotesque gesture of contempt. A knot, like an enlarged Adam's apple, obtruded at his neck where a strip of blanket was tied. Knowing, but wanting to disbelieve, his eyes traced the strip up to the bar where it was tied. His stomach cartwheeled. Beyond doubt, Tom Daly was free of the burdens of this life now. Those demons he'd feared had won. A great void opened inside Henry. The devil drug dealers had helped Tom down the path which had turned this small cell into his coffin.

Henry sat there with the body as the sun came in through the bars announcing a day his friend would never see. He glanced wearily at Tom's bed, noticed a note lying on the pillow which still carried the imprint of his friend's head. He rose languidly, forced his mind to focus on the baby scrawl. Tom had written, 'Sorry for the trouble, Henry. This gypsy needed to be free.'

With the note in his hand, he stumbled to the door, pressed the buzzer. He was thinking how once it could easily have been him lying there if he hadn't met the right people who'd helped him climb out of his own pit of despair. Why hadn't he been able to save Tom?

Officer Smith opened the door, an irascible look on his face. When he saw the body, the look changed to one of horror. He took a step backwards and shouted for help. Another officer soon came running, his shoes echoing in the corridor. Both squeezed in to the cell together. Henry didn't look at them, just sat motionless, staring at the floor as though he was seeing all the way down to Hell itself.

'My God,' Smith proclaimed, edging forward, not sure of the situation, eyes all over Henry to ascertain he had no weapon.

The other officer didn't move. The blood had drained from his fat face, leaving behind an impression of a white blancmange to which nose and ears had been added as an afterthought. Smith edged back to the door, touched his shoulder.

'Go and ring for the doctor. I'll stay here. We can't move him yet.'

The other officer, glad to be away, rushed back down the corridor.

'We'll be moving you to another cell, Torrance,' Smith said. 'You won't be getting out in the morning. This mess will have to be cleared up.'

Henry glared at him, his eyes on fire. 'He wasn't a mess. His name was Tom Daly and he was a human being – more human than you.'

Smith dropped his eyes. Sensing Henry might snap and he had no back up, he made no answer.

*

Three days after Tom Daly's death, on a sunny day tempered by a north east wind, Henry stood at the prison gate. They'd detained him three extra days, but it was clear he had no part in Tom Daly's death and they'd informed him of that fact as though they were awarding him a merit mark. The screw opening the door for him was one of the better of the breed, coming up to retirement soon, looking forward to it. Another kind of release, Henry supposed.

'Good luck to you, son. Keep those fists to yourself and you'll be fine.'

Henry gave him a half smile, couldn't stretch it to a full one because Tom was on his mind. The fact that his pad mate was lying cold on a mortuary slab had taken a great deal of the gloss off his big day. They'd questioned him about Tom, probing for reasons behind his suicide but he hadn't given much away, didn't tell them about the drugs, nor about the incident in the shower. No doubt they'd found evidence of drugs inside Tom and no doubt there'd be a fuss about how he'd procured them, the buck passing between departments to salve consciences. But nothing would change. People like the Jacksons would still hunt down the weak like jackals. And he didn't feel free of guilt himself. He could have told them who had supplied Tom Daly, didn't because grassing was anathema ingrained in his psyche.

As the door opened, a gust of wind blasted through, slapped his face, ruffled his hair. The screw withdrew his key, laughed as he stepped aside to let him out.

'Big Man in the sky trying to tell you something,

Torrance, eh? Telling you you're better off inside, maybe.'

Henry gave him a wry glance. 'A wind in the face is better than a stab in the back. There's plenty inside there would do that sooner than look at you – and that's just the screws.'

The door shut behind him, the noise like a book slamming shut in the funereal quiet of a library, a welcome finality to it. Henry was carrying a parcel which contained his few belongings. The prison car park was fifty yards away. Beyond that lay a desolate, open space, and further off than that nothing but industrial buildings and warehouses. Henry remembered watching a television programme about a lion released into the wild after years in captivity, its first tentative meanderings. Right now, he felt he could identify with that beast faced with vistas to explore after the confines of a cage. As he strode forward, he hoped he'd have half the courage the lion had shown.

He intended to walk the three miles into Middlesbrough, then get a bus to South Bank. After half a mile, he was suddenly conscious of a car behind him matching his speed. He turned to find Mary sitting behind the wheel. She flashed him a smile, braked and wound the window down.

'Hurry up and get in,' she said, grinning. 'I don't want to be done for kerb crawling.'

Henry glanced up and down the road. Thankfully it was deserted. He climbed into the passenger seat and pulled the door shut, didn't say anything as she pushed the car into gear, just sank further into his seat and raised his jacket collar.

Mary checked her driving mirror, then, with a twinkle in

her blue eyes, looked across at him.

'Who are you hiding from, Henry?'

He didn't laugh. They'd agreed to keep a low profile. Mary, bless her, had chanced her arm already and he was only minutes out of prison.

'Anyone could have seen you,' he said. 'Then where would you be? You'd lose your job, wouldn't you? You think I want to be responsible for that?'

She tossed back her hair, focused on the road ahead. 'Libraries are dull places. I've got to have a little risk in my life.'

'Driving me to an exotic back street in South Bank isn't exactly an adventure to die for, is it?' He realized he'd sounded a real grump, added more gently. 'But it's a nice thought and I am grateful.'

'At last,' she said, 'a little appreciation. I had to take a few hours off work to do this you know.'

Henry let the matter drop and soon they were talking in a relaxed way, recapturing the ease that they'd found with each other from their first meeting. His eyes wandered intermittently to the surrounding landscapes. Time had been chiselling away, defacing places which held memories for him, but what surprised him most was the sheer volume of traffic on the roads. Traffic seemed to be coming at him from all directions like swarms of bees. He'd forgotten there were so many people in the world.

Mary took the ring road around Midddlesbrough, came off into South Bank. The place had changed, but not as much as he'd geared himself to expect. He detected a change in Mary's mood when she drove past a row of derelict houses standing like sad survivors of a bombing raid and surrounded by the foundations of those already demolished. Pock-marked walls were decorated with graffiti telling the police how much they weren't loved, bestowing crudities on local individuals and rival football teams. Further off, like sentinels guarding the fires of Hell, rotund chimneys with fat lips blew smoke clouds into the sky. Welcome to South Bank, Henry thought.

He sighed. 'It was never your actual Utopia but it's got worse. I knew people who once lived in those ruins, good people too.'

She didn't reply and he directed her to the house his aunt had left to him. He was relieved to see the whole terrace was still standing.

A gang of hooded youths was loitering on the street corner. When they saw the car, their heads swung in its direction. Henry could see Mary was troubled by them. He wasn't enamoured himself. The way they were looking it was like being sized up by predators anxious for fresh meat.

From the outside the house was just as he remembered it and he silently thanked his aunt for her generosity, for saving him from having to enter a hostel. Mary glanced in her mirror at the gang on the corner, opened her mouth to say something, hesitated, then came out with it.

'Look, you don't have to stay here. You can come and stay with me in Yarm.'

Henry glanced in the mirror, saw the gang was still watching. Living with Mary in Yarm, the best small town in the North-East, was tempting and he figured most men would have leapt at the chance. But they'd been over this and he hadn't changed his mind. He smiled and let it go.

43

'I'd ask you in,' he said, 'but the probation officer will probably call and I don't trust that lot back there to leave your car alone. They know it doesn't belong here.'

'My God,' she said. 'It's like prison if you need to be looking over your shoulder. I'm worried for you, Henry – and you're avoiding the issue.'

He sighed. 'We've been over this. I've nothing to offer you, Mary. Let me settle for a while, try to get a job, get used to everything. What if I can't cut it and mess up your life as well as my own? You'd lose your job and – maybe we won't work out.'

She narrowed her eyes and he could tell she was annoyed.

'Sounds like you haven't much faith in us, or any need of me.'

He avoided the eyes probing his, drew in a deep breath. 'I've got faith in you and I do need you. It's me I'm doubting. It's all very well me talking. Five years is a long time. I've been institutionalized and need to break out of that mould, prove myself to myself. You can see that, can't you?'

She was silent for a minute, fingers drumming on the steering wheel.

'OK,' she said, finally. 'I can see what you're driving at, but aren't you making it harder for yourself coming back to a place with more than a passing resemblance to Beirut?'

'I'm familiar with the area. There are good people here and I have a chance of work, like I've told you.' He stared hard into her eyes. 'I don't want to lose you, Mary. You're everything to me and that's another reason why I don't want to leach off you. I'll get on my feet, be my own man.

44

You've got to let me do that.'

Mary seemed to relax a little. He thought he'd convinced her but she wasn't finished with him yet.

'Your father and brother didn't contact you for five years, did they?'

He shook his head, wondering where this was going. 'Not a word. They're strangers to me now.'

Mary cocked an eyebrow.' You're sure of that? Your father lives on the site. Coming back here isn't about pride, is it? A perverse need to prove yourself to them?'

He hadn't thought of it like that, but now he wondered if, somewhere in his subconscious mind, that was part of it.

'Well, pride maybe. Everybody needs their share. As for my father and brother – it's a good theory, but I doubt it.'

Mary glanced at her watch. 'Look at the time. I'd better get going. I'm due in soon.'

Relieved that particular conversation was at an end, he leaned towards Mary, kissed her on the cheek.

'Thanks for understanding. I want it to work out for us, Mary, believe me I do.'

She smiled across at him. 'Perhaps you're right. We'll give it time. Meanwhile – you be careful.'

As he started to get out, she opened her handbag, took out a mobile phone and handed it to him.

'Just a little present from the modern world. Use it to keep in touch.'

He thanked her and watched her drive down the street past the gang of youths. He blew out his cheeks. South Bank had made a bad impression on Mary, no doubting that. But there were good people living here, he was sure. He intended to gravitate towards them. The crimes he'd committed in his teenage years had been few and petty, mainly when he'd allowed himself to be led, believing gypsies had to stick together. It had taken prison to mature him. Now, he wanted to be an individual, not a follower.

He let himself into the house, made a quick inspection. It was adequately furnished, clean and, though small, a palace compared to his cell. On the kitchen table, he found a note from his probation officer telling him he'd find tea bags in the cupboard, milk and a few supplies in the fridge. That was an unexpected and welcome touch. When he'd made himself a cup of tea he took it through to the living room, lowered himself into an armchair, and put his feet up. His thoughts then turned back to Mary, how easy it would have been to have gone to live with her in Yarm. He'd upset her, but he was convinced he was in the right. He didn't want to be the kind of man who went to a woman he loved with nothing to offer.

John Walsh kicked idly at a stone. He'd been out of school five months, longer if he counted that last year when he'd never managed a full week's attendance. The transition from schoolboy to school-leaver hadn't been a watershed for him, hadn't felt like a rite of passage into young adulthood like the films sometimes made out. The lives of the five mates, who stood with him near the entrance to an old church, had followed a similar pattern. He watched them now with their hooded tops, stolen designer trainers and attitude, wondering what the future held for any of them. Already they had two friends who were dead, both from drugs. No one in his group had been able to get steady work, were hardly inclined to look anyway. Three of them he'd known since infant school; he could still recall their chubby-faced innocence in those far off days. Now, those same faces had a pinched, feral look. He worried that he might look the same, but doubted it. Miraculously, though he kept company with them, he'd kept off hard drugs, so he figured his looks weren't quite in their league when it came to a beauty contest for zombies. His future worried him though. Boredom was circling him like a shark, in ever decreasing circles, taking another bite out of his confidence as each monotonous day passed. There surely had to be more to life than hanging around on street corners day after day.

Barry Tonks, the leader of this bunch, nudged him in the ribs, breaking into his reverie.

'What's up, Walshy? You look like someone's just offered you a job.'

'His last job was at MacDonalds,' one of the others chipped in. 'But he turned veggie. Couldn't even cut the mustard.'

To laughter all round, a third joined in, 'Couldn't squeeze it on, could you, Walshy? Kept missing. Just couldn't hit those burgers.'

John joined in the laughter. At least the banter broke the boredom. Barry Tonks laughed louder and longer than the rest. John didn't mind that. Barry would never push it too far with him, as he often would with the others. If it came to a fight, the outcome would be uncertain. Barry knew that, couldn't risk losing. He liked to be the big man and that was fine as long as he left John in peace. Tonks was the leader and that was fine too. John didn't want to be a leader but he didn't want to be on the outside looking in either. In South Bank, loners had a hard life. You were either in or out. If you didn't belong to a gang you had nothing and there were plenty of other gangs willing to make your life hell. It came down to either join up or get out of town. But where could you go?

'Why are we waiting here, Barry?' John asked, glancing at the church. 'Going to rob the vicar, are you?'

Barry stuck out his jaw. His tone was as malicious as the look that came into his eye.

'One of my runners has been playing up. I've heard he passes here round about now.'

John sighed. Barry was a drug dealer. His runners were school kids who delivered the merchandise for him and collected his money in return for a pathetic remuneration. It kept him out of the spotlight and, as long as the kids behaved themselves, reduced the risk he would be caught. His own supplies came from someone higher up the chain. John hated the fact he was using young kids, but nothing he could say would alter the facts of life. Tonks was making money, far more than any of them, and he liked to show it off. In an area where there wasn't much about, the money gave him respect amongst his peers. Woe betide anyone who tried to interfere. He'd cling to his empire like a dog to a bone.

Minutes later the target of Barry's anger rode round the corner on a bicycle, head down, concentrating on controlling the bike so didn't see the gang until he was almost upon them. When he did look up, he saw his fate awaiting him, applied the brakes, but couldn't stop the forward momentum. Tonks grabbed the handlebars, brought the bike to a halt and the boy shrank back away from him, flinching as though expecting a blow. It never came. Instead, Tonks' arm snaked out, grabbed his collar, hauled him off the bike and pushed him up against the church wall, held him there like a chicken about to be plucked.

'Sorry, Barry! Sorry!' the lad croaked.

Barry shook him. 'People ring me, tell me my little postman didn't deliver. What are you trying to do to me? Tell me you didn't lose the stuff.'

The boy shook his head frantically. 'I was ill, Barry. Honest! I'm gonna do it tomorrow.'

'So you didn't lose the stuff. That's good. But what about the punters waiting with my money?' He leaned closer until he was right in the boy's face. 'Punters who trust me, but get edgy without their sweeties.'

Barry let go of the boy's throat, smiled down at him. The boy misinterpreted his actions, thought he must have been forgiven and risked a smile of his own.

Barry lost the smile, turned to his audience.

'Little runt needs a lesson. Maybe I should dump him in the River Tees.'

One of the others said,'With a concrete life-jacket, eh, Barry?' He winked at the group. 'Like you did to that other kid who disappointed you.'

The kid's face blanched. John felt sorry for him. He figured he couldn't have been more than twelve and was terrified.

'Ha'way, he's just a kid, Barry man.' he said, reluctantly. 'Look at him! He's wetting his pants. He won't let you down again.'

Tonks turned and glowered at John. The rest of the gang

shuffled their feet, maintained an edgy neutrality. This was business. You didn't interfere. Cardinal rule! Walshy should know better.

'There's no such thing as a kid in South Bank,' Tonks said in an angry voice aimed at John. 'They're all grown up by the time they're five, old when they reach his age.'

'But he's learned his lesson,' John said. He knew he was pushing it, hoped Tonks would see sense and let it go.

Tonks shifted his gaze back to the boy, eyed him up and down like an angler weighing up his catch, wondering whether to throw it back in, or eat it for supper. He turned back to John.

'You're part right. He's learned his lesson and he is just a scrawny kid, so he'll just get a slapping to remind him to keep an eye on the ball – my ball.'

Without warning he slapped the kid hard across the face, drew his hand back ready to deliver again. John looked away, told himself the kid had known the rules. He'd done his best to help him. What more could he do?

Henry woke on his first morning of freedom luxuriating in the novelty of a soft double bed, the absence of prison sounds and the privacy his own house afforded. Last night he'd been content to stay in and watch television, had no desire to go out and paint the town red like most of the cons on their release. He knew men who had gone wild that first night, channelled all their stored up emotions into an orgy of drinking and other excesses, then committed another offence and woke up back behind bars again. Once, he might have wanted to celebrate like that, but he had no desire to do so now. It was enough to be free and know Mary was there for him.

He rose late, made himself tea and toast and decided to wander down to the local spa, buy himself a few treats he'd missed. A fat cream cake sounded good and maybe a big wad of cheese. Pile on the calories, son; he'd learned from deprivation there was much pleasure to be had in the small things. He'd maybe buy a paper, read it at his leisure.

He set off at a fast pace, came round a corner thinking about that cream cake. A gang of hooded youths, like the ones that had been on the street corner yesterday, had gathered near the church. Henry checked his stride.Gangs meant trouble, were unpredictable, were best avoided. He decided to cross to the far side of the road and already had one foot off the pavement when he noticed one of the youths was holding a small boy up against the church wall. The boy was cowering, trying to protect himself but the youth holding him knocked his arms aside and slapped his face.

Henry's hackles rose. Father Andrew had told him to walk away from trouble, not hazard his probation. When the youth struck the boy for a second time, that advice went right out of his head. His anger impelled him towards the gang. One of them noticed him coming, hauled his hands out of his pockets and said something to his mates. The youth delivering the blows must have heard it because he held back the third blow and looked in Henry's direction.

All the gang were watching Henry now. As he halted two yards away, he could see curiosity in their eyes. Who was this guy with the effrontery to approach them? Was he going to provide them with a bit of fun? They were measuring him up, could see he was a big guy but adopted confident poses, sure that five of them were enough to deal with whatever he could bring to the table.

Henry eyed the big, ugly one who had been doing the slapping. 'You should be ashamed of yourself,' he said, his voice calm.

He let his gaze travel over the whole group, mouth and nose curling in distaste, as though they had crawled out of the nearest sewer and he could smell the stench coming off them. 'You lot, too, for watching him attack a little kid who can't hit back.'

It was best to adopt a direct approach sometimes, as though you had no fear in you. He'd learned that in prison. He hoped he'd said enough to shame them into backing off. Violent confrontation was the last thing he wanted, but he was ready for it.

With an amazed expression, the youth let go of the kid. Arms encircling his upper body, as though he was hugging himself for comfort, the boy slid down the wall trying to stifle his sobs.

The youth stepped away from the wall, went up on the balls of his feet. His head moved side to side like a snake gearing itself up to strike. His eyes shifted incessantly between Henry and his mates. Henry read the signs; he'd seen them before in men priming themselves for action. This one needed to maintain his kudos, couldn't afford to back down and lose respect. It was looking bad.

'You're a big man,' the youth said, finally. 'But big don't mean brains.'

With that, he reached inside his jacket. Sun glinted on steel as a blade appeared in his hand. Henry kept his face impassive in spite of the dry feeling in his mouth, the acrobats performing in his stomach. The knife had escalated the situation in the blink of an eye.

'Can't count to five, big man, eh? Long odds for you, all of us!' the youth snarled. He waved the knife in the air. 'But you do know this ain't for cutting bread.'

'Let's do him, Barry,' one of the youths called out, feeding off his leader.

Barry took a step forward. Henry could see the crows' wings etched into his upper cheeks below the eyes. The eyes themselves were cold, black depths, devoid of feeling. Henry had no doubt that, like his erstwhile pad mate, Tom Daly, this youth was a user, living on an edge as sharp as the knife in his hand.

He focused on Tonks and nothing else as he stooped and picked up the fallen bike. Then, he glanced at the tearful boy.

'Yours, son?'

The kid wiped his tears, realized this was his chance and pushed away from the wall. He grabbed the bike from Henry, climbed on and, legs pumping like pistons, pedalled off.

Almost as an afterthought, before he disappeared around the corner, he called over his shoulder,' Thanks, mister!'

A silence descended. Henry wanted to turn, walk away. He'd achieved his purpose: the boy had escaped. What stopped him was that knife and the madness in those eyes. If he turned his back, Tonks might well plunge the weapon between his shoulder blades, or thrust it into his ribs. He decided he'd have to concentrate on putting the leader down quickly, in the faint hope that would make the others back off. If you cut the head off a snake, so the saying went, the body became useless.

'There are no heroes allowed in South Bank,' Tonks said. 'Hasn't been since Mannion played for the Boro – that was in the Ice Age.'

'There's only scum like us now,'one of the gang cackled. 'Welcome to the cesspit.'

Brandishing the knife, Tonks spoke in a sing-song voice, 'The smoggy men are going to get you.' That gave his pals much amusement.

He started to advance. Two of the other youths drew knives ready to back him up. Henry's throat constricted, felt so dry it was as though sand was pouring down his windpipe. He didn't think he had much of a chance. He'd either be killed or end up in a casualty ward severely injured. Any second now, they'd be on him like a rash.

Then, suddenly, one of the lads who'd pulled a knife shoved it back into his waist band.

'Pigs,' he hissed.

Tonks came out of a crouch, neck stretching like a nosy housewife eyeballing new neighbours, looked beyond Henry. With a groan of frustration he slid the knife under his top and retreated a few steps. Henry risked a glance over his shoulder, saw a police car cruising down the street.

The vehicle slowed to a crawl. The shaven-headed copper in the driving seat wound down the window and gave them a disdainful once over as he passed by. None of the youths moved a muscle but their eyes watched Henry, waiting for him to flag it down and squeal blue murder.

Henry was more than tempted to flag the car down. But it went against the grain, against the code he had lived by for five years, and back beyond that. Grassing had been a taboo in both the gypsy encampments and in prison and old habits died hard. That aversion apart, it would look bad being involved in confrontation so soon after his release. So the moment came and went and he did nothing. As soon as the car disappeared up the street, the knives appeared again so quickly he had no time for regrets.

Tonks started to advance as though nothing had happened, just a delay in the proceedings. Henry decided he'd just made one of the biggest mistakes of his life.

'Let it go, Barry man,' a voice protested. 'He could have whinged to the coppers, couldn't he? But he didn't say a word.'

Henry glanced at the tall, blond youth who'd spoken up. He'd noticed him earlier, standing back as though reluctant to be involved.

'He earned a chance, Barry man,' the youth continued. 'He didn't grass. Just think about that a minute. They'd have searched us, found knives on us, maybe more.'

For a moment, a cord of tension seemed to stretch between the leader and his challenger. Finally, Barry let his gaze drift to the others who seemed to be waiting to see which way the wind was going to blow.

Meanwhile, the blond youth turned to Henry with a puzzled expression.

'Tell us why you didn't you stop that car, big man? You had your chance there.'

Henry decided to keep it simple. 'Old habit. The way I grew up. You didn't grass.'

55

The blond turned to Barry. 'See, he's like us. Call it even, man. One favour for another. He could have had us in the police cells by now. Show him some mercy in return.'

His gaze left Barry, embraced all of the others. 'It takes a strong man to show mercy – a big man.'

None of them said a word, seemed content to remain neutral and let the two of them decide. Barry knew those words about mercy and strength had put him on the spot. Maybe mercy wasn't so important, but he didn't need anyone doubting he was strong.

'Kings show mercy in those old films on telly, so maybe he has a point,' he said, lowering the knife.

The blond faced Henry again. This time there was a hard edge to his voice.

'Stay out of other people's business, mister. Today you've been lucky. Don't go thinking you can cross my friend Barry and get away with it again. You're new around here, so learn quickly.'

Henry knew when Lady Luck was smiling on him, didn't say anything in case it might change her mood. With a nod of gratitude to his saviour, he turned quickly on his heel and headed back the way he'd come. Once he was back inside the house, he made a mug of tea to calm his nerves and wondered why, once again, he'd had to get involved. Perhaps Mary was right and he shouldn't have come back to South Bank. He had to hope today's trouble was a one off and nothing like that would happen to him again.

When Mary picked him up that evening he took the decision to keep quiet about his confrontation with the gang because it would only worry her. They intended to have a bar meal in the Bluebell in Acklam. The route took them past the caravan site where he had once resided and where he knew his father had settled down. Memories came flooding back to him.

Mary noticed his preoccupation. 'So that's where your father lives.'

He didn't say anything, just nodded assent.

'No desire to see him?'

Mary's question took him by surprise. She knew how he felt. Why did she want to stir the pot when she was aware the contents had gone rotten a long time ago?

His reply was bitter. 'You mean in the same way he's had a burning desire to see me all these years?'

She kept her eyes on the road, didn't answer immediately. He hoped she was going to leave it there but she didn't.

'He is your father, Henry.'

He snorted, angry at her persistence. When he'd told her all about himself, he'd thought he'd made his feelings about his father and brother crystal clear.

'You haven't got a clue, Mary. You can't imagine the way we lived. Your life has been so different.'

'He might have changed.' She waited a few seconds. 'Was he really so awful?'

He turned his head away from her, not wanting her to see how angry she was making him. Only when the fire inside him died down, did he allow himself to speak.

'My mother died when I was twelve. That's when he unfurled his colours. He drank more, was bad-tempered most of the time, occasionally beat me – hard. Only now, when I'm grown up, can I see how selfish he was. The final straw was when he and my brother got me that illegal fight – to make money for themselves.' Henry sighed. 'I was naïve, didn't know what they were getting me into.'

'I can't understand why they didn't visit you. It seems so—'

'Selfish and callous,' he snapped. 'They say when you're in trouble you find out who your friends are. Well, that applies to family too. And I found mine ran for the hills – didn't exist.'

Mary finally let it go and there was silence. He looked out of the window to the mid-distance where the Cleveland Hills rose above the landscape, the dregs of the evening sunlight adorning them with golden haloes as the first shadows of night crept across the fields to touch the hems of their robes. The world was turning, would turn forever. What good was his bitterness? Yet how could he forget?

He looked at the view from the other window. Teesside's industrial edifices loomed there, gigantic shadows in the fading light. He could see wisps of smoke rising from the silhouettes of the chimneys like signals aimed at gods of the sky. It was such a contrast to the view of the hills, heaven and hell juxtaposed, a metaphor for the soul of man. Henry sighed; life was a mystery. All you could do was put one foot in front of the other and keep hoping you weren't wandering down the wrong road.

'The hills are beautiful, aren't they?' Mary commented.

He smiled, made himself lighten up. 'Beautiful, like you, yes. The sun on those hills, the woman I love next to me. I know what I've been missing.'

She laughed. 'Far too poetic. You're not that romantic.

You'll have to cut back on your reading.'

He laughed along with her. Was he wrong not to tell her what had happened that morning? He thought about it again, decided he was right first time. She'd just try to get him to move, to go and live with her before he was ready.

Arriving at the Bluebell, they parked the car and headed for the lounge. Mary insisted on buying the first drink so he sat down and waited while she went to the bar. He found it strange to be surrounded by groups of people of both sexes, the cheerful buzz of conversation all around him. Prison had been sociable in its own way, he supposed, but always there had been the knowledge that they had lost their free will, their lives under the control of others. He half expected a prison officer to appear on the scene at any moment to break up the happy little groups with a suspicious scowl and an announcement that association was over for the day. He smiled, relishing the fact that, at last, he was a free man and nothing like that was going to happen.

'You should smile more often,' Mary said, returning with the drinks and placing them on the table.

He grinned up at her, took a sup from his pint and smacked his lips as the liquid slid down his gullet reintroducing itself to his taste buds. A pint had always been a pleasure but, unlike his father, he always had known how much was enough. Noticing the posters round the wall announcing future entertainments in the pub, he pointed them out to Mary.

'I can read those now,' he said. 'That's down to the education staff and yourself, Mary, for helping me to read. Deep down I was ashamed.'

She leaned over, touched his hand. 'Not your fault,

Henry and it was nothing to be ashamed of anyway. Changing schools all the time, you never had a chance.'

'My father didn't help much. He thought it was all a waste of time. "Not for the likes of us", he would say.' Henry sighed, took another sup from his glass. 'Didn't want me to be able to do something he couldn't, I guess.'

He was enjoying his drink, thinking this was the life. Mary was as easy to talk to outside prison as she'd been inside those grim walls. No doubt about it, his luck had definitely changed when he'd come across her. One time he'd wondered if the attraction was because he was incarcerated and she was one of the few women with whom he had any contact, but he knew whatever it was between them went far deeper than that, came from the soul, whatever that was. For him, the miracle of it was that she was willing to take a chance on him knowing he was a jail bird.

They chatted, then ordered meals at the table. Halfway through his ham and eggs, Henry happened to glance towards the bar. The piece of ham he speared never made it to his mouth. He sat there motionless, staring ahead, eyes bulging. It was as though in his mind he was watching a pleasant landscape suddenly overwhelmed by black clouds, thunder rumbling ominously in the background, with the certain promise of a lightning strike to follow. Mary looked up, noticed the change in him.

'What is it? You look as though you've seen a ghost.'

His nodded towards the bar. Puzzled, she followed his gaze, realized then why he had felt no need to explain what he'd seen. The man standing at the bar had a definite resemblance to Henry, except he was a bit older. He was staring back at them, a sardonic twist to his lips. She turned to Henry again.

'That, my dear, is my beloved brother.' He spat his words as though they were so distasteful he wanted to be rid of them.

Mary said,' Of all the bars in all the world—'

'It's no coincidence,' Henry told her.' You can be sure of that. This isn't his kind of establishment. Sawdust and spittoon is his style.'

'He's coming over.'

Frank carried his drink with him. That sardonic grin was still there as he scratched the back of his head with his free hand and looked down at them.

'Can't believe my eyes. My little brother just back from' – Frank hesitated, glanced at the surrounding tables, checked himself – 'his holidays – and already he's out with a bit of stuff. Fast work, kid.'

Henry's eyes blazed with annoyance at the insult to Mary. Afraid he might start something, she reached out under the table, gripped his knee. The moment passed.

'This place has too much class for you, Frank,' he replied. 'But you couldn't wait to see your little brother, eh! Managed to ignore him for five years, suddenly got fraternal urges.'

'Fraternal, eh! Big word that. Don't know what it means.' Frank shook his head. 'We decided to let you do your growing up alone, kid, like you'd joined the army or something. That way you learn faster, become a better man for it.'

Henry screwed his face up in disgust. 'My father and you are a pair. It wasn't the army, was it? What if I was drowning in there?'

Henry's voice had risen and a few heads were turning. Frank's eyebrows came down and he shifted his gaze to Mary who had been listening to their exchange without interfering.

'I've business to discuss with you, Henry,' he said, added with an emphasis that was clearly for her benefit, 'family business.'

Henry snorted. 'Family business! That's a new one. Anyway, this lady's more to me than any family. There's nothing she can't hear.'

'It's all right,' Mary said, patting his arm and rising. 'I'll go and stretch my legs.'

Henry wasn't pleased. He wanted to tell his brother to get lost but he knew Mary wouldn't want a scene so restrained himself. Frank slid into the chair Mary had vacated leaned back, tilted his head to one side and scrutinized his brother.

'You're looking in good condition,' he opened, his affable tone at odds with the sly look that crept his eyes. 'We heard you used the gym in the – rest home.'

Henry was taken by surprise by. His father and brother hadn't bothered to make any contact yet knew he'd kept training. He figured there must be an ulterior motive lurking because they'd not been concerned about his welfare. Then he remembered what Tom Daly had told him. Could it be his brother's purpose here was to size him up for a return to the fight circuit? That would fit with the Frank he remembered. Well, if that was what was lurking behind those sly eyes, he was going to be disappointed.

'Body and mind, Frank! Body and mind.'

'What?'

'Fit in body and mind, Frank. That's me. Used the gym like you say, but got myself some education too. Bet you didn't know that. A fit mind in a fit body? That's the thing – like the Greeks said. You have to have the balance right, Frank. You should try it. Make a man of you.'

Frank frowned. He was annoyed at his brother's baiting but he didn't bite, just changed the subject.

'You haven't asked about the old man.'

Henry picked up his beer, took a swig, as though he needed time to ponder the statement, swirled the glass in his hand until a froth formed.

'Let me think,' he said eventually, with affected puzzlement. 'Old Man, you say? Do I have one? Seem to remember I did once, but the mind plays tricks, especially when you're in a – rest home, you called it.'

Drumming his fingers on the table in irritation at Henry's deliberate obtuseness, Frank carried on regardless.

'He's not a well man. Not the man you remember.'

Henry sighed. 'You're dancing me around the ring, Frank. I'm tired and bored. Get to the point. This is five years on. I'm not a gullible kid anymore.'

'He's made a big mistake, your father.'

'Don't we all. Not looking for sympathy, is he?' Henry jabbed his own chest. 'Not from this direction, surely?'

Frank held up his hands. 'OK! I'll get to the point. He put out big money arranging a fight with the latest Jackson to make a name for himself. Daniel, Jet and Terry approached him when he was on the booze, hurt his pride saying things about you. They took advantage of his state of mind. I had to stand by and watch it happen.'

Henry grunted. So Tom Daly had been right. This conversation was going to end up where he'd expected it to. Frank was just taking the country route.

'There's no fool, like an old fool. Why should I care?'

Frank stared at a spot on the table. He looked more worried in that moment than Henry had ever seen him.

'The Jacksons put up forty grand and he matched it.'

Henry didn't let his surprise show. His brother was laying his cards on the table one at a time, like a gambler slowly revealing his hand. Henry had an idea which card was coming next, decided to pre-empt him.

'Let me guess,' he said, stroking his chin as though it was a matter that deserved great thought. 'All this must have taken place at Appleby Horse Fair.'

Frank smiled a bitter smile, shook his head. 'So you know? In that case you'll also know who the old man was backing.'

'I got it from a gypsy in gaol who ended up hanging himself because the Jacksons got him hooked on drugs. They get around those Jacksons, don't they, Frank?'

Frank's chin dropped. The slyness had gone out of his eyes but it had been replaced by an equally unattractive desperation. It came pouring out of him.

'You've got to fight. The old man's life savings will be gone if you don't. The caravan would be all he had left. He's not a well man.'

It was the nearest to pleading he'd ever heard from his brother. But Henry could only feel resentment towards him. He'd vowed that he would never be involved in an illegal fight again. Frank, who with his father had fixed that last, fatal, fight, was showing no respect at all for his feelings. It was as though the past five years had never existed and he could walk back into Henry's life expecting his younger brother to revert back to his old self at the drop of a hat. It felt so unreal perhaps any moment now he'd awake, find he was back in his cell dreaming it. His first night out with Mary had certainly been ruined by his dear brother.

'I won't fight for you, for my father, or anyone else,' he growled.

Frank's eyes sent sparks across the table. 'You'd let the old man down in his hour of need?'

For Henry, the irony, to which his brother seemed totally oblivious, was salt rubbed in old wounds.

'All these years neither of you have given me a thought,' he fired back. 'Beats me how you've got the nerve to sit there and ask me to do anything for the old man or you. And I thought prison porridge was thick stuff, Frank.'

Frank glared at him and Henry recognized the ruthlessness in him. He was certain he'd be sifting through all the options now until he found the one that would carry maximum effect. He'd always found it hard to take no for an answer, his lovely brother.

He leaned forward until he was so close Henry could see the furrows on his brow and the small scar on his nose which he had given him in a childhood fight.

'There's too much riding on this. I can't take no for an answer. You will fight, Henry. I'd prefer you did it the easy way but – there's other means of persuasion.'

Henry was boiling but tried to retain his cool.

'That's more like my brother,' he said. 'Good job I didn't

expect a family party.'

Frank shrugged, pushed his chair back and stood up. He put his hand in his pocket and placed a piece of paper on the table.

'My number. Ring me. I'll give you a week or two's grace. If you're not on side by then it'll get hotter and hotter – until you melt.'

Henry sat very still looking up at his brother. The threat had been delivered in tones so cold and distant it was as though he'd been announcing train times over a tannoy. He'd always had a streak of stubborn selfishness and ruthlessness, but there was a new quality to him in that moment that touched on evil. Or had it just taken time away from him for Henry to see more clearly what had always lurked?

'Go to the Devil, Frank. He'll recognize his own.'

Frank shrugged his indifference. 'Start training, Henry. Do it for your father's sake. If that doesn't float your boat, think about your share of the money.'

With that, Frank turned on his heel and wove his way through the tables, heading for the door. On the way he knocked someone's drink over, but carried on without an apology, ignoring the protests that followed him. Henry watched it happen and it seemed a fitting finale to their meeting – Frank, in character, brushing all considerations aside to get where he wanted to be.

A range of emotions, mainly outrage, assailed Henry. His own brother had threatened him and he had no doubt it wasn't an idle threat. He suspected there must be more to the business than he was being told. Frank had been present when his father had been set up, hadn't he? It wasn't in his nature, surely, to sit and quietly watch as they fleeced the old man. Those thoughts were interrupted when Mary returned.

'Was it that bad?' she said, wrinkling her nose. 'You look like you've just lost a pound and found a penny.'

He mustered a half smile. 'You're not too far off the mark.'

'He offered you money?'

His half-smile turned cynical. He decided she might as well know the gist of it.

'He's got a fight arranged for me, my dear brother. The prize money is eighty thousand – winner take all.'

Mary's hand rose to cover her mouth. Her eyes widened in dismay, and then concern came into them.

'You're not—?'

'Of course I'm not. I told him to get lost. Can you believe the brass neck on him though?'

As though she'd received a physical blow, needed a second to recover from the shock, Mary closed her eyes. When she opened them, she reached out to him, rested her hand lightly on his arm in a supportive gesture.

'I'm proud of you, Henry.'

'What for? There was no choice.'

'But there was. You resisted the money. Many wouldn't have.'

'The money didn't come into it. I learned my lesson the hard way. Bare knuckle is primitive. My only excuse is that I was ignorant back in the day.'

They bought a fresh drink and sat there another hour. Henry considered telling her about the money his father had gambled and his brother's parting threat, but he decided not to. It would make a bad night worse. Instead, he tried to lighten the conversation, salvage some joy from their first evening out. Hard as he tried, though, he couldn't shake off the memory of that malicious look on his brother's face.

Mary drove him home and parked outside the house. They arranged to see each other the next night and, since it would be Friday and she wouldn't have to go to work on Saturday, she managed to cajole him into agreeing to stay over at her place. He kissed her goodnight but hesitated before getting out of the car.

'You know someone from your work is going to see us together eventually and it'll get back. The Bluebell wasn't exactly secluded.'

'You're more worried than me,' she told him. 'There are other libraries who'd take me on. I've made enquiries already.'

'Don't think it's not hard for me,' he said. 'But I've told you my reasons.'

He watched her drive off, then went inside and straight up to bed. All that had happened in the last few days replayed in his mind as he tried, unsuccessfully, to sleep. More than an average share of trouble had come his way and he had to concede Mary had a point when she'd suggested that coming back to South Bank wasn't the brightest of ideas. One thing he couldn't have anticipated, though, was that his own brother would cause him grief. Though he was determined he wasn't going into an illegal fight, what kept nagging at him was that his brother liked his own way and, for sure, didn't issue idle threats.

*

Next day, early afternoon found Henry standing outside the community centre remembering his boyhood and the part Michael Lane had played in his life. Inside this building he had received his first lessons in how to box according to the amateur rules. Micky had seen his potential, shaved the raw edges off his unsophisticated style, curbed his tendency to advance at all costs, his frequent loss of temper. The building was an old church that had seen much better days, but Henry knew it had a heart. What went on inside was what really counted, made a difference. Whenever his gypsy family had spent time in South Bank, Micky had been like a father to him, attempting to instil values that would keep him out of trouble. It had taken time and distance for him to realize how hard Micky had tried with him. It wasn't that he hadn't listened, more that contact with the trainer had been intermittent, broken by long spells on the road where it had been easy for a young boy to forget and drift off the path.

When he opened the door it was like stepping back in time. The boxing ring was the centrepiece, surrounded on all sides by training equipment where the young boxers were at work. Familiar sounds drifted to his ears; fists beating out a tattoo on the punch bags, the sharp sound of breath inhaled and exhaled like steam trains gathering speed, the clink and rattle of weights as they vibrated on contact with the hard floor. Had he really been away so long, he wondered? He spotted Mick at the back of the hall, near a door to another part of the building where Henry remembered more cerebral pursuits were on offer.

He walked down the hall, past the ring and stood a yard

behind Micky who was in the process of reading the riot act to a shamefaced looking youth who had obviously transgressed. He smiled to himself as he waited, recalled times when he'd been on the end of one of Micky's tongue lashings.When the youth was dismissed, he spoke out.

'Never turn your back on an opponent. Always be aware. It only takes a second.'

The old trainer didn't turn around and Henry thought he'd taken him by surprise. But he was disabused of that notion when he spoke in that familiar gruff voice of his.

'Blue sweatshirt, jeans, a stone heavier.'

Henry laughed. It was exactly how he was dressed and he held up his hands in defeat as Micky turned to face him. Only an extra wrinkle or two around the old boy's eyes told of the passage of time. His seventy-year-old body was slim, not an extra ounce on it. If it hadn't been for the shock of white hair, he could have passed for a man ten years younger.

Micky pulled Henry into a bear hug, that show of affection taking him by surprise. He felt his eyes begin to moisten, hoped it didn't show when they broke apart.

'Saw you the moment you stepped in the door,' Micky said. 'What's been keeping you, son? Father Andrew told me you were getting out two days ago.'

'Just coming back down to earth,' Henry told him.

Wise eyes assessed him. 'And you couldn't find a better place to do that than Slaggy Island, eh?'

Slaggy Island was another name for South Bank. It was used more by the old-timers and referred to the nearby slag heaps created by the steelworks. Henry avoided the question, grinned as he glanced around at the young lads who were exercising hard.

'I hear you might be prepared to let me loose on your latest protégés.'

'Could do with help,' Micky said. 'You know boxing. You know what I stand for. What this place is about.'

Remembering his illegal fights, Henry went red. Micky saw and understood why. He grimaced, swiped the air with his hand in a dismissive gesture.

'Look, son, the past has gone. I tried to warn you about bare knuckle but you were just a kid. There was good in you, you know, otherwise I wouldn't have let you through those doors, then or today.'

Henry looked down, shuffled his feet. 'You know how much I regret – how grateful—'

Mick gripped his arm, stopped him right there. 'Let's go into the kitchen, have a brew. I can keep an eye on things through the hatch and we can have a chin wag.'

As soon as they were settled in the kitchen, Henry poured his heart out to the old trainer, in a way that he had only done to Father Andrew in the recent past. He told him about the fatal fight, his disappointment with his own family and his determination to live a good life. Mick listened without interrupting, his eyes leaving Henry only occasionally to check everything was OK in the hall.

'So it was an unlucky blow that killed him,' he mused, when Henry finished. 'And a delayed reaction because he didn't go down immediately?'

'That's right,' Henry confirmed. 'We heard the police coming and everybody ran for it. There was chaos and he staggered off on his own. They found him dead in a field fifty yards away.' Henry glanced down at his hands. 'A blow to the temple killed him and my blood was all over him.'

'But it was an accident, wasn't it?' Mick said, his voice gentle.

Henry shook his head. It was no good Mick trying to make him feel better. He knew that he'd struck a blow that had killed a man, intentionally or not, in an illegal fight for big money.

'It was manslaughter, Micky. If I'd been wearing gloves, it would never have happened. You warned me enough times about illegal fighting but I listened to my father and brother instead.'

Henry placed his mug on the table, put his hands together, intertwined his fingers as though he was about to say a prayer of contrition.

'The worst of it,' he murmured, in a voice made forlorn by regret, 'is that I totally lost it. He hurt me and everything you told me about always keeping cool, boxing scientifically, went out of my mind.' Henry lowered his head. 'The animal came out and pure hate surged through me, the desire to destroy him at all costs.'

Henry met Micky's eyes. The old trainer's face didn't show anything and he didn't move a muscle.

Henry continued, 'To know that I have that in me, what it can do, is a terrible thing.'

'We all have that in us, son,' Micky said, staring at the wall behind Henry, as though in his mind he was looking back at his own life. 'That night you just looked further into the abyss than most ever do.'

Henry clasped and unclasped his hands, finally came out with it. 'Isn't it hypocritical to teach boys control in the ring when I lost it like that? Not exactly a good example of how to control yourself, am I?'

Mick answered him in measured tones. 'Just the opposite. You've been there and so many of these lads are just a step away from it. You know why discipline is vital. Boxing can give them that discipline and it channels all that wild energy that they'd use on the streets otherwise.'

Henry nodded. 'I know what you're saying. If you think—'

'I do think! Just come in when you can and lend a hand.'

Henry smiled. 'Fine, just fine.'

'Good, that's settled then. Now tell me what else has been happening to you.'

They chatted for another twenty minutes and by the time they'd finished Mick knew everything that had happened to him since his release.

'It bothers me, Micky, how trouble seems to be around when it's the last thing I want or need.' He sighed, dolefully. 'I'm frightened I'll lose it again. Yet I still charge in.'

'It'll be different when you've settled,' Mick told him, 'and to help you do that I think I can get you a job that's right up your street.'

'I certainly need to be employed. What exactly is it you have in mind?'

'An ex-South Bank lad made a lot of money,' Mick explained, 'and he makes regular contributions to help keep this place going. Right now, he's starting a sanctuary for mistreated horses. I've had a word and he'd start you working with the horses three days a week on a trial basis, employ you full time if everything works out.'

Henry felt a surge of gratitude towards his old trainer. Perhaps the cards were falling his way at last. Horses were a great love of his. Mick had remembered that.

'Sounds ideal. I won't let you down, Micky.'

'It won't pay well, you know.'

'Beggars can't be choosers. It ain't easy for an ex-con to get work. Besides, I intend to study in my spare time, improve myself.'

The old trainer smiled. 'Good on you, son. My money's on you succeeding. Now, let me show you around this place. It hasn't changed that much. Just getting older like me.'

Mick led him round the main hall and Henry had a word with the lads. It was obvious they were keen which would make it easy to work with them. Finally, Micky took him through the door to the classroom at the back. The rather dingy rooms Henry remembered had been converted into one big one with a bright, fresh ambience. There were computers along one wall, all in use. In the centre, a middle-aged woman with a pleasant motherly face was seated at a round table with a group of teenagers. She smiled when she saw them.

'She's a volunteer,' Micky explained. 'We have several who come in and help the lads with numeracy and literacy. Quite a few of the boxers attend.'

Henry grinned. 'I take it that requires a bit of subtle persuasion from certain quarters.'

Micky scratched his head. 'Subtle? I don't know the meaning of the word.'

They were leaving the room when Henry caught a glimpse of a youth sitting at the computer in the furthest corner of the room. He could only see his profile but his hair was blond and he was nearly sure it was the lad who'd spoken up for him during the street altercation. He pointed him out to Micky.

'Is he a regular here?'

'Spasmodic,' Mick answered. 'Potentially a good boxer, but flits in and out. Sits at the computer sometimes to try to improve his English but flatly refuses to sit with the groups. John Walsh is one of my failures, truth be told. Yet, he's no real trouble so I let him come in when he wants to.'

Henry considered Mick's summary of the youth's attitude, then said, 'Mind if I go over and have a word?'

Micky shrugged, 'Go ahead. He's a bit like you were. Maybe he'll recognize a kindred spirit.'

The youth didn't notice Henry's approach. His face was set in concentration and his lips were moving soundlessly as he stared at the screen. Henry stood behind him for a moment before speaking.

'Remember me, son?'

The youth spun around as though he'd been caught doing something he shouldn't. His face flushed and he looked startled. Then recognition dawned and he tried to hide his embarrassment.

'You're the feller with the yearning to visit a hospital.'

Henry grinned. 'And you're the feller who stopped it happening.' He added quietly. 'I'm going to help Micky out from now on, son.'

A disappointed look came into the youth's eyes. 'Going to throw me out, then?'

' 'Course not. You did me a good turn. Like to repay you.'

The youth frowned, gave Henry a quizzical look. 'Would have cost you ten quid to the hospital and back by taxi if you'd survived, so ten quid would do it.'

Henry laughed at his cheek, then said,' Why won't you join the others?'

The youth's face changed again. His lower lip protruded and there was something akin to fear in his eyes, as though he had a secret he had to keep at all costs.

'I'm not a divvy,' he said, peevishly. 'That's what my mates would call me if I sat in one of those groups.'

Henry understood where he was coming from. He'd been there himself so knew how delicately he'd have to handle this.

'They're not divvies, son,' he said, evenly. 'And neither are you. That's just a name insecure people use about others to make themselves feel better.'

The youth looked at him and shrugged. An uncomfortable silence descended. Henry decided in for a penny in for a pound and persisted.

'I've been exactly where you are now. I trained here when I was a kid and didn't take all the opportunities I was offered and now wish I had.'

A flicker of interest showed in the youth's eyes. He cocked his head to one side. 'So you're saying you can't read or write?'

'I can now, but there's room for improvement. Like you, I tried to teach myself but it wasn't until I had a teacher that I progressed.'

The youth flicked a stray blond hair out of his eyes, looked Henry up and down as though he was measuring him for a suit.

'You look like a boxer.'

Henry nodded. 'I'm going to help with the coaching and training. Micky tells me you're not half bad.'

'I do a bit when I'm bored,' the youth said, with another nonchalant shrug.

Henry decided, though the ice hadn't entirely melted between them, a few cracks were developing. It was worth taking a chance.

'Look,' he said, 'I'll teach you reading, here or at my place, maybe both. I can remember how I was taught and it'll work for you if you stick it out.'

Doubt clouded the youth's eyes. 'You're not a perv, are you?'

The words stung Henry, but he managed to control his temper.

'How long does a perv last in South Bank? Get that idea right out of your head fast.'

'But people don't do owt for nowt, do they?' the youth said, his forehead furrowing.

Henry sighed. 'In my book, one good turn deserves another. Then there's always karma.'

'Karma?'

'Karma means what you do, good or bad, comes back on you. I could do with some good karma in the bank so you could say my reasons are selfish.'

The youth fell silent and for a moment Henry thought he'd lost him. Then he spoke.

'I'll learn quicker, you say?'

'At first it's like pushing a rock and you'll think you can't shift it. But suddenly it'll move and you'll be on a roll, picking up the pace. That first effort is important and after that you have to persist.'

Henry knew from the youth's intense expression he was taking it in but was still hesitant. He decided to press him.

'What have you got to lose, son? There's not much round here for you right now except wasting time.'

The youth scrutinized him, his eyes intense. Henry knew he was looking for ulterior motives, wondering how much trust he could invest in a stranger. He thought he was going to lose him until he nodded and spoke up.

'You're right. I've nothing to lose.'

'Good,' Henry said, not a little surprised. 'I'll find the right books to help you and we'll make arrangements.'

'This is just between us, right? None of the lads you saw me with need know.'

'None of their business, is it?' Henry said. 'They won't hear it from me.'

After that conclusion, they made arrangements for the best times to meet in the centre, then Henry left him at the computer and went to find Micky. John Walsh hadn't exactly been effusive. Henry surmised that was because he'd been let down in the past, was reserving judgement. He told Micky about it and the old trainer seemed pleased.

'There are plenty more where he came from,' Micky said. 'Maybe you can take on an extra role as a teacher.'

'Don't know about that,' Henry said. 'Think this one will be a handful.'

Micky laughed. 'You should know, son. You can start here tomorrow if you like. Peter Fairbrother, the guy starting the sanctuary, is on holiday. Soon as he's back home, I'll take you to his farm and introduce you.'

Henry's heart went out to the old-timer. In this environment, he was feeling better already and the job sounded ideal. He knew there were college courses in equine studies that might suit him. But that was jumping the gun. For sure, he'd be kept busy, not moping around depressed with his lot, looking back at the past with bitter regret. He'd be no good to Mary like that.

'How will I get out to the farm, Mick – that is if I'm acceptable?'

'Don't worry about it. There's a local feller works out there. He's agreed to give you a lift and you can borrow my car if you ever need to.'

Henry smiled. 'You've covered all the angles for me, Mick.'

Mick walked with him to the door. They agreed he would come in whenever it suited him. On the threshold, Micky shot him a quizzical look.

'You don't have the desire to box again yourself, do you, son?'

Henry shook his head. 'Be a bit like putting my hand back in the fire, even with proper boxing.'

Micky drew in a breath, let it out slowly. 'Pity that, but understandable – very understandable.'

'My aim is to settle down to a nice quiet life with my lass,' Henry stated. 'I just hope trouble doesn't keep knocking on my door.'

'Hold your breath and think twice if it does.'

As he walked down the street, Henry thought about those words. It was easier said than done and he hoped he wouldn't be tested.

*

Henry held two pads in the air while a young lad danced in front of him throwing punches. Occasionally, he shouted a word of advice about the lad's footwork or his combination punches. Two weeks had passed since that first conversation with Micky and he'd been happy. He found his involvement with what went on in the hall rewarding. A bonus was that John Walsh had come to him every day, visited his house as well. Under Henry's tuition he had made progress and in the last lesson there had been a brightness in the lad's eye that he hadn't seen before. Henry thought, with a bit of effort, he could catch up on the lost years. In a way, it was a bit like looking at a mirror image of himself, those first sessions of prison education. But there was a long way to go yet. Many a seed fell by the wayside, or was strangled by jealous peers.

Henry told the lad he'd done enough on the pads, set him to work on the weights. As he was walking away, he noticed a figure near the door he recognized. Barry Tonks, the gang leader who had given him trouble, was leaning against the wall, arms folded, staring in Henry's direction. His lip was curled into a sneer that made his disdain of the activities going on around him very clear. A moment ago, Henry had been thinking how contented he was with his life. Now, as though to rebuke him for his complacency, he sensed trouble on the horizon in the form of the gang leader.

Micky wandered over, stood beside him. He was looking at Tonks, his face thunderous.

'That lad's banned,' he rasped. 'He's a known drug dealer and poison for the boys in here. I'll have to turf him out.'

'He was the leader of that gang I told you about,' Henry told him. 'I'd better help you.'

'You're better out of it for your own sake,' Micky told him. 'Just keep an eye on what happens. He might try it on, especially if he has his mates hanging around outside.'

Without any show of haste, Micky walked towards Tonks. The boxers stopped what they were doing, their eyes following him. They all knew Tonks shouldn't be there, that Micky was about to confront him.

Henry shouted, 'Get on with it, you bunch of old women.'

The lads resumed their activities but kept glancing towards the door. An air of expectancy hung in the air. Henry felt it, that sense of imminence, the same as when two boxers enter the ring. He knew well enough how an individual with a bad attitude could create vibrations. There were plenty of psychopaths in prison who'd had that effect, enjoying the sense of fear their unpredictable moods instilled in those around them, revelling in the sense of power it gave them. He figured Tonks was of that ilk.

Henry couldn't hear what Micky was saying but he was right in Tonks' face, showing no fear as he gesticulated towards the door, leaving no doubt in the youth's mind, nor in those watching, that he wasn't welcome and had to leave the hall. The gang leader stood his ground and pointed across the hall at Henry. Mick put up a warning finger, a gesture that made it clear to him that he hadn't to move from that spot, then strode back to Henry.

'What's up?' Henry asked. 'Need help?'

Mick waved his hand dismissively. 'Not to deal with him. Not when he hasn't got his gang. But he says he has a message for you from some guy he met, said he'd leave as soon as it's delivered. I said I'd ask you if you wanted to receive it.'

Henry frowned his puzzlement. 'We have no mutual acquaintances so what's he up to?'

That was enough for Micky. He started to turn, ready to go back and finish what he'd started. Henry restrained him.

'I'll hear what he has to say, then thank him nicely and tell him to leave. Save you dirtying your hands.'

Micky lowered his eyebrows. 'You sure? You've already had a tangle with him once and you can't afford trouble.'

Henry glanced at Tonks. The gang leader was affecting an air of nonchalance for the benefit of onlookers, hands in pockets, lips pursed, whistling to himself.

'Looks calm enough,' Henry said.

'Sure,' Micky growled. 'Calm like a snake in the grass. Be on your toes.'

'Used to that,' Henry said and started to move.

As he drew near, an insolent smile played on the lad's lips. Henry halted, stood feet apart, arms folded, dispensed with preliminaries.

'Let's hear it.'

'You're not going to like it.'

Henry sighed. 'You're just the monkey, kidda. Don't know who the organ grinder is, but I don't suppose he expects his monkey to speculate about my feelings.'

Tonks' face flushed. The mockery in his eyes vanished. His face grew vacuous as he searched for the smart reply and couldn't find one.

Finally, he said, 'Feller who gave me the message looked

a bit like you, but was better looking, harder looking.'

Suddenly Henry knew, would have bet money on it. Frank! His heart sank.

'So what?' he said, trying to hide his feelings. 'Bit feminine, isn't it, to notice another man's looks?'

'Feller told me to tell you,' Tonks paused there, let his eyes drift around the room, trying for dramatic effect, 'that this place is a fire hazard – would burn like tinder.'

There wasn't a doubt in Henry's mind that the message had come from Frank. His breathing accelerated. How foolish he'd been to think there was even a chance his brother would give up. The supercilious expression on Tonks' face only served to stoke the fury mushrooming inside him. As he struggled to contain it, the youth saw the hardness coming into his eyes, sensed the storm gathering, realized he was right in its path. He became wary.

'Like you say,' Tonks' tone had changed to defensive now. 'I'm just the messenger.'

He'd barely finished when Henry's arms snaked out, spun him round and forced his arm up his back. He ran him to the door, bundled him through. The boot on the backside was the final indignity for his bruised pride.

'Don't come near this place ever again,' Henry shouted.

He was aware that all eyes were watching him as he walked back inside. In spite of the earlier instruction, the lads had stopped what they were doing and were staring. Micky wasn't moving either.

'Just get on,' Micky bellowed. He placed an arm around Henry's shoulders, spoke quietly, 'Must have said something bad to get you riled like that.'

Back in the kitchen, Henry decided only the truth would do for a man who'd done so much for him. He repeated the message, said he believed it must be Frank's strategy to get him to fight, and that he believed he was capable of carrying it out. Mick listened stone-faced.

'So now you know why I manhandled the creep,' Henry said, 'and why I'll have to finish here.'

Mick was quiet for a moment, thinking it out.

'The lads here saw you stand up to Tonks. They'll admire you for it. If you leave now what does it tell them?'

Henry shook his head. He understood what Micky was saying but he didn't want Micky's life's work going up in smoke because of him.

'Believe me, I don't want to leave. I'm happy here. But there's no other way.'

'No arguments, you're staying,' Micky said. 'We can take precautions. Chances are it was a bluff.'

Henry saw, from the adamantine look in his eye, Micky meant what he was saying but he was still doubtful. It was a big chance to take.

'I'd like to get the police onto him,' Micky mused. 'But if the lads here saw the police around they'd class me as a grass and they'd stop coming. You know how it goes around here. That aside, Tonks would deny everything, plus you laid your hands on him and that would put you in hot water.'

Henry leaned back in his chair. 'The Wild West revisited. No law this side of the Tees. You have to do things for yourself.'

'But taking the law into your own hands would be a breach of your parole. Be careful, Henry.'

'Point taken. At least I held myself back. Didn't give him the hiding he deserved.'

'We'll have to watch that brat Tonks,' Micky grumbled.

'But you're sure you're happy for me to stay on?'

The trainer pulled a face. 'You don't think you're the first to have trouble here, do you? A number of the lads have come under threat, one way or another. We've usually sorted it, or it's just blown over.'

Mick saw the concerned look on Henry's face.

'Look, son, I've never backed down to that type and I'm too old to start now. Once you do it opens a floodgate and you're done for.'

'But you've worked so hard to build up this place. It's been your life.'

Micky sighed. 'It's more than just a building, son. I like to think it stands for something, so do as I say and quit worrying about it.'

Henry smiled his appreciation. Beneath that smile, he was still worried. A few years back Mick had a reputation as a hard man, hard but fair. But he was older now and the world had changed. Now a dispute was more likely to be settled with a knife in the back, literally or metaphorically, rather than with fists.

Frank parked the Mazda and watched Barry Tonks in his driver's mirror as he shambled along the pavement like a gauche child denied his sweets. A empty lager can that lay in his path received short shrift, a petulant swing of his boot sending it into the road. His actions brought a smile to Frank's face. A few minutes ago he'd watched another boot, his brother's, making contact with Tonks' backside as he'd been thrown out of the hall. That had pleased Frank because it meant he'd rattled Henry's cage, just as he'd intended when he'd sent Tonks with the message.

Frank leaned across as Tonks drew level with the car, opened the passenger door so that it blocked the youth's path. The gang leader, who had been in a dreamland imagining all sorts of revenge against Henry Torrance, pulled up short.

'Still in orbit, are we,' Frank said, gesturing for him to get in beside him, 'or just got a pain in the backside?'

Tonk's didn't like the levity and it showed. Lips protruding sulkily, he climbed in. He sat hunched up staring out of the windscreen, not looking at Frank. The gypsy wasn't sure whether that sullenness was meant for him or stemmed from a malevolence he was brewing in his heart against Henry. Whatever the cause, he would use the youth's anger; it would make manipulating him much easier.

'You can't afford it,' Frank said, shaking his head.

At last, Tonks looked at him. He was pouting and his eyebrows were down so his features were crowded together, as though a weight was sitting on his head squashing his face. Frank thought he looked like a Neanderthal.

'What?'

'Loss of face,' Frank said, amusing himself.

Tonks couldn't look at him, started to fiddle with his hands. 'I delivered your message, didn't I?'

'It'll get around that he threw you out. Your punters will get to thinking Tonks ain't so hard so we can take advantage. Before you know it, you got challengers on your turf – I can't afford that.'

Tonks looked perplexed. 'But you sent me to him. Why, if—'

'Thought you were up to it,' Frank said, cutting him short. 'Why I paid you.'

Tonks gripped the dashboard with both hands, dug his fingers in. Monkey face, monkey's grip, Frank thought and wondered about his brain.

'You giving me the push?'

Frank gave him his benign smile. 'The situation isn't irretrievable, Barry. I'll keep you on the books, son. But you'll want another job, won't you, one that'll hurt that feller, help you get back on that pedestal?'

'I'd love that,' Barry said, his face at last unfurling.

'Good lad. I'll let you know then.'

Barry started to get out of the car but Frank reached across, grabbed his arm.

'That lad, Walsh you told me about, I think he'd be good in our line of work and I need another seller. Sound him out, eh!'

'He's never been interested.'

'Try him. I'm expanding. He won't interfere with you.'

Barry Tonks was relieved to hear it. The bottom lip that had started another sulky droop made a retreat. He got out and leaned back inside.

'Thanks for keeping me on.'

Frank winked and started the engine. 'Just remember who butters your bread and you'll be fine. You'll be hearing from me, kidda.'

As he drove away he watched Tonks through the mirror thinking there was one born every minute and good job too. The bottom of the pile was as far as people like Tonks were going and they made a good, soft cushion for him to sit on.

John Walsh was on a training run, blowing hard, sweat running down his back. He hadn't realized how unfit he'd become until the big man had given him a couple of boxing lessons, left him labouring like an old man. Now he was running daily, trying to build his stamina, enjoying it more than he thought. His efforts to improve his reading and writing, combined with his fitness sessions, had introduced a routine to his days, alleviated the feeling of drifting rudderless on the streets. The big man said he was young enough for a fresh start if he made the effort, and he trusted him.

As he reached his house, he looked up at the sky. Perhaps his mother was somewhere out there in the universe, looking down on him. It was a nice thought. One thing for sure, she'd be pleased he'd turned down the offer Tonks had made for his boss two days ago. Tonks thought he should consider it an honour to be asked. John didn't consider it that, was mystified why he had been asked to join the ranks of drug dealers.

He let himself in the front door, checked his father wasn't home then made for the kitchen, figuring to make himself a meal while he cooled down before his shower. Afterwards, he'd tackle the homework Henry had given him.

The blast of cold air on his face when he opened the fridge was welcome. His taste buds were already at work; yesterday he'd done the shopping, bought bacon, eggs, sausages, chips, so was looking forward to a fry up. But he discovered the fridge was empty, apart from two lonely sausages and half a dozen chips sitting in the middle of a large plate, an insult even to a serial dieter. John heard his stomach rumble, protesting at the meagre repast set before it when it had been expecting a feast.

His father! He'd done it again, brought his friends home after a drinking session and they'd demolished what would have lasted two days. Why had he even bothered to leave anything? Were the sausages, sitting there in their splendid isolation, some kind of message designed to let him know who was boss? He wouldn't be surprised if it wasn't his old man's idea of a joke, so that he couldn't be accused of not leaving him a sausage.

Deciding he'd have to make the best of it, he put the kettle on and shoved the plate in the microwave. He'd fill up later with jam and bread, as long as the gods were smiling and his father hadn't denuded the pantry of all things edible. When the kettle boiled, he made tea and cut the sausages and chips into smaller pieces and sat down. He tried to eat slowly to make each mouthful last.

Half a sausage and a chip were gone when he heard the front door open. He groaned inwardly. That would be his father. If he was lucky the old man wouldn't come into the kitchen and he'd have peace to eat.

He knew that hope wasn't going to be fulfilled when he heard a noise behind him and a shadow fell across the table. He turned to see his father's burly frame filling the kitchen doorway. Father and son stared at each other without words. Even from a yard away John could smell alcohol, could see the glazed, absent look in his father's eyes, as though an alien had insinuated itself into his body. His old man raised an arm, stabbed it in the direction of the plate.

'You're eating my tea,' he slurred. 'My s-sausages.'

His old man could be aggressive in drink. Through bitter experience John could read all the signs, knew he was looking for a fight and, in that mood, even a sausage could be an excuse for one. It would be better for him just to leave the kitchen. Yet he was nursing a sense of indignation, hard to quell. Against his better judgement, he set it free.

'You and your spongeing mates have eaten two days' food. You never thought about what I would eat, did you?'

His father lurched forward towards him, put a hand on the wall to steady himself. His head was bobbing. Blue veins, like ink lines, bulged in a face red from drink.

'You're the sponger here,' he snarled. 'Jus – a para-site, you.'

John felt his temper rising. He warned himself to control it but it kept on bubbling under the surface.

'Like father, like son, is what they say, isn't it?'

His father's eyes narrowed to slits. He leered at his son.

'Your mother made you soft,' he said. 'Me, I worked until I was made redun-dun-dant.'

'Aye, and that was ten years ago,' John fired back at him. 'You aren't fit to speak my mother's name either. Don't think I don't remember how you treated her. She was too good for you, my mother.'

John had gone too far and knew it. His father came off the wall, threw a punch which, more by luck than judgement, caught him on the jaw. Even in drink his father was a powerful man and it knocked him sideways. He landed on the floor, stars dancing in his eyes. When he recovered his senses, his father was standing over him.

'That's where little slug-sh belong,' his old man slurred.

John shuffled away from him on his backside, used the sink to haul himself to his feet. The pain in his jaw made him want to strike back, to hurt his father the way he had hurt him. Spinning in a vortex of anger, he drew his fist back to strike. But then another thought flashed into his mind, the lesson he'd been learning in those boxing sessions with Henry, the emphasis on self-control outside the ring as well as in. He realized he was in danger of losing all control, and lowering his arm slowly to his side, he turned away from his father and made for the back door.

As he exited, he heard his father shout. 'Teach you to eat my saus-saush.'

He waited in the back yard for a moment, drawing in deep breaths as he tried to calm down. Then he went into the alley, started walking, no idea where he was going, just wanting to be as far away from his father as possible.

He walked quickly, hoping physical effort would help, worrying how close he had come to unleashing his fury. Resentment at the beatings he'd received had been building like a torrent in his soul. Today that torrent had been on the brink of overflowing. Could he guarantee that next time it wouldn't break its banks? His mother had faced up to his father for him many times; paid the price, too. Four years ago she'd died, and since then he'd had no one to help him through, nowhere to go for respite from his father's moods.

He'd walked half a mile when a flurry of rain brushed

against his cheek. The flurry developed into a downpour, rain bouncing off the pavements like an army of little devils throwing itself against the concrete in kamikaze attacks. John ran into a bus shelter which had just enough roof left on it to give him cover as he stared out at the bleak day. How he wished his mother had lived and found the courage to take him away. No doubt about it, one day matters had to come to a head with the old man. When they did he'd have to leave home. But where would he go?

Just as he'd resigned himself to sheltering until the heavens relented, a car drew into the bus bay and Henry Torrance wound the passenger-side window down.

'You look like someone with time on his hands.' Henry said. 'Fancy a run out to the country? Micky's driving me out there on business. You're welcome to come with us.'

Managing a half smile, John stepped out of the shelter and climbed into the back of the car. The incident with his father was bubbling away at the back of his mind, but he was grateful to be out of that bus shelter and in the comfort the car.

'Where are we going?' he asked, trying to sound chirpy but conscious of the false note in his voice.

Henry laughed. 'Believe it or not, we're going to see a man about a horse.'

'More than one horse, and they're all damaged goods,' Micky chipped in, adding as an afterthought, 'You know, like some people are damaged.'

'It's a sanctuary,' Henry elaborated. 'A farm where they take in horses who've been mistreated. I'm hoping to get some work there.'

With a wistful air, John said, 'They should have places

like that for humans.'

Henry and Micky picked up on his tone of voice, exchanged glances.

'You OK, son?' Micky asked.

'Yeah! Just don't like this weather.'

Henry pointed ahead. 'Looks like there's a break in the clouds where we're headed.'

'You're not going to give up the coaching, are you?' John suddenly asked. 'If you get the job, I mean.'

Henry shook his head. 'Probably I'll do more in the evenings, less in the days.'

'That's good, then, because I need your help with my lessons if I'm going to get anywhere.'

Henry turned to look at him. 'You don't think I would give up on you now, do you?'

They were out in the country, approaching Great Ayton, a small town near the Yorkshire Moors. John had a vague memory of being there before, many moons ago with his mother. They drove through an avenue of trees and the sun burst through the grey veil of clouds. Everything was suddenly brighter, as though a dusty painting had been wiped clean to reveal colours in their full glory. They turned onto the track that led to an old farm building which had been tastefully renovated so it retained a certain rustic charm.

'Peter Fairbrother's done well for a South Bank lad with a poor start,' Micky said when they were out of car, 'and he's never forgotten where he came from.'

Off to their left was a field with a barn. Three horses were grazing there, their long necks stretching gracefully to crop the grass. The field was surrounded by green woods. To John, it was a picture of calm serenity, so different from South Bank. He thought Peter Fairbrother was a lucky man to have escaped to this.

His thoughts were interrupted when a tall man, with a ruddy, weatherbeaten face and an aquiline nose with a ridge where it had been broken, emerged from the house and approached them with a jaunty stride. Micky introduced Peter Fairbrother to Henry and John.

After preliminary pleasantries, the farmer said,'Well, we know why we're here so we might as well take a stroll and I'll introduce you to the horses. They're the important ones.'

As they walked the farmer talked passionately about his desire to help mistreated horses. Currently, he could only cope with six animals, but this was only the initial stage of his project and he intended to have twenty or more. Already he'd been inundated with requests to take more and he was determined to release another field for the purpose as soon as possible.

The horses were grazing near the barn. They raised their heads and two of the three, obviously wary of the humans, trotted off, settled at a distance. The third, a chestnut, ambled towards them. Peter Fairbrother stretched out an arm and stroked its nose.

'He's fourteen,' the farmer said,'and he's a friendly old thing even though he has every reason to hate anything that walks on two legs.'

Henry ran a hand over its flanks, paused at three long scars that ran like tram lines from the horse's shoulder to its belly. He screwed his face up in disgust.

'Done with a machete,' the farmer explained. 'The owner was a bad-tempered drunk who took it out on the horse.

That was his final *coup de grâce*.'

John felt a rush of sympathy for the old horse. He reached out, stroked its nose. It looked at him with its gentle eyes, thrust its head forward and nuzzled his neck.

The landowner laughed, took a carrot from his pocket and handed it to John.

'Slobbery old thing, ain't he? Doesn't do that to just anyone, you know. He obviously likes you. Give him this and he'll be your friend for life.'

John held the carrot out. The horse took it and started munching.

'How could anyone—?'

Fairbrother pointed to the other horses. 'The black over there was blinded in one eye and had his belly slit. The grey was left in a field until it nearly starved to death.'

A melancholy silence fell on the group. It was hard to accept that men of flesh and blood like themselves could do that.

'If you decide to employ me,' Henry said, breaking the silence, 'what would be my duties.'

'Mucking out, ordering food, liaising with the vet. As we expand, I'd expect you to look at damaged animals for me, assess their condition, arrange for them to be transported here. Mick tells me you know horses, so I'd rely on you a lot.'

'Sounds good to me, but it's only fair to tell you I've no formal training. I was brought up with horses. They were part of my life until—'

'Yes, I know,' the farmer said, saving Henry from embarrassment. 'Micky's opinion is good enough recommendation. As for qualifications, I'm a self-made man with no qualifications myself.'

Henry looked him in the eye. 'I won't let you down and I won't let the horses down. I like what you're doing here.'

'That's it settled then,' Fairbrother said. 'Let's head back to the house, and go over a few details.'

They strolled back to the farmhouse. John kept looking back over his shoulder. There had been something about that old horse that had struck a chord with him and he was reluctant to leave. He was glad the horses had a bit of peace in their lives. It meant there was hope in the world and he wanted to believe in hope.

Back in the house, Mrs Fairbrother, a tall, willowy woman with dyed blonde hair and a reserved frostiness in her manner that contrasted with her husband's open demeanour, served them tea and scones and made little attempt to respond to efforts to draw her into conversation. John was hungry and wolfed down two scones.

After tea the farmer walked to the car with them and noticed John taking a last look at the horses.

'Bring the lad with you whenever you want,' he told Henry. 'He seems to like it here.'

Henry turned to John. 'You up for that?'

'Love it,' John said, and thanked the farmer.

'A satisfactory day,' the old trainer said when they were back on the main road, 'except for the cold spell.'

Henry looked across at him, puzzled.

'Cold spell?'

'The blonde ice queen. Peter's a good sort but I think his wife would like to wear the trousers. Those were the vibes I got.'

'You think she disapproves of me?' Henry said, not

referring directly to his criminal past because John was there, but knowing Micky would catch his drift.

'Could be, son. I'd keep away from her if I were you.'

'Got you,' Henry said. 'No worries there.'

That night Henry was in Mary's flat for the first time. They'd enjoyed an evening at the pictures and were sharing a bottle of wine. The wine loosened his tongue and he was telling her about his day, how much he was looking forward to working with those horses.

'I'm sorry,' he said, thinking he was talking too much.

Mary misunderstood. 'I've told you to stop worrying about being here. I'm a big girl. They can only sack me, not incarcerate me.'

Henry shook his head. 'Not what I meant.'

Mary sipped her wine, her eyes sparkling over the rim of the glass.

'Apologies accepted. Whatever the offence committed, no matter the gravity.'

She was in a good mood. Henry laughed, feeling his own life was on the up at last.

'I've talked about horses all night,' he explained. 'Talking a load of manure, probably.'

'But it's interesting manure,' she said,' and I'm glad to hear there are people like Mr Fairbrother around.'

'It won't pay much,' Henry mused, 'even if I work full time.'

Mary looked at him, face in serious mode. 'I'd rather you did something you liked than be well paid and miserable.'

'That's how I see it.'

He considered how lucky he was that Mary was warm and wise. Maybe five years of prison life was a price worth paying to have a gem like her come into his life. Was the wealthy Peter Fairbrother, whom he deemed a good man, as lucky with his woman, he wondered?

'That brother of yours hasn't bothered you again?' Mary suddenly said.

The change of subject caught him by surprise, made him hesitate. He'd decided not to tell her about Barry Tonks visiting the hall because he didn't want Frank's shadow looming over another evening. But she had asked him outright, was looking him straight in the eye, and he didn't want to lie to her. With some reluctance, he told her what had happened and about the threat he was sure had come from his brother.

'He wouldn't dare,' she said, eyes wide with amazement.

Henry shrugged. 'It wouldn't surprise me.'

Mary pondered it for a moment, shook her head in denial. 'It would be too risky for him – I mean – arson.'

'When there's money involved some people will do anything and one sure thing is that my brother likes money.'

'But it's your father's money involved, isn't it? Not his.'

'Ultimately Frank's, when the old feller dies. Apart from my share that is, though as far as I'm concerned he can keep it.'

Mary bit her lip. 'You haven't seen your father yet?'

'You know how I feel about that.'

'Maybe your father would take a different point of view, wouldn't condone Frank's behaviour. After all, people change.'

'In his case,' Henry said bitterly, 'that's too big to swallow, be like snow in summer.'

Mary tilted her jaw at him. 'You should go see your father. What happened at Appleby Fair is hearsay. Even if it's true, your father might not know what your brother's doing to you – might call him off.'

Henry's feelings went too deep on the subject. He found it difficult to hide his scorn for her optimism. She didn't know his family.

'Nice people like you, Mary, always believe there's a good streak in the worst of us and all you need is to find the right button to press.'

Anger flared in her eyes. He wished he'd adopted a different tone, not used her as a target for his frustration.

'Don't patronize me, Henry, especially when you don't really believe what you're saying – when your own actions belie your words.'

Henry blushed. 'What exactly do you mean?'

'John Walsh! You think you can help him, don't you?'

'That's different!'

'No, it isn't! Your father must have some good in him, surely?'

Henry fell silent. He didn't like arguing with Mary even if he thought she was way off the mark as far as his father was concerned.

'Point conceded,' he said finally. 'But any good in my father is buried deeper than North Sea coal so what good is it?'

'Look,' she said, 'I took a bit of a chance on you and don't regret it. Maybe you should face your father, give him a chance to explain himself.'

Henry felt a little ashamed because it was true she had

taken a big chance on him. In a sense, she still was.

'I'm sorry,' he said. 'I was bang out of order talking to you like that. My only excuse is any mention of my father, after the way he let me down, messes with my head.'

'Facing him just once, getting it out of your system, might do you a power of good.'

'I'll think about it, Mary.'

She reached out and took his hand. 'At least that's progress. Let's go sleep on it before you change your mind.'

'Yeah!' he said, 'Let sleeping dogs lie for now, eh!'

John Walsh was leaning on the gatepost waiting for his father to leave the house. Since the battle of the sausages, he'd done his best to avoid him. Their conversations were little more than an exchange of grunts. So little that was meaningful passed between them, John figured at times he might as well be living with the original caveman.

He let his gaze wander over his surroundings. The three houses opposite were unoccupied, downstairs windows boarded up. Like alien invaders from subterranean depths, weeds grew from cracks in the pavement. Two skips, overflowing with rubbish, stood on the road. They reminded John of landing craft sitting on a beach in a war zone. Looking lonely, an old settee leaned against one of those skips, its springs erupting from the cushions. John sighed. This was home and he'd have to put up with it. But why did some people settle for less in life? Circumstances, money, a host of reasons he probably couldn't guess at? Whatever, he was going to do his best to get out before the place sucked him down into the swamp as it had done so many others. He'd made up his mind about that.

'All right there, kidda.'

The voice brought him out of his daydream with a jolt. He turned his head to find Barry Tonks standing two yards away. If he needed it, the gang leader's presence was a salutary reminder of his present circumstances and that dreams were a long way from reality.

'All right, Baz,' he said, straightening up.

'Cushtie, mate,' Tonks answered, with a cocky roll of his shoulders implying how could it be otherwise when he was the big man around here. He started rubbing the back of his neck. John knew Barry's habits well enough to know that meant a question was coming his way.

'My man's been asking again,' he said finally. 'Told me to give you another go, said things change for people.'

John stared at the house opposite where the glass in an upstairs windows was broken in spider's web patterns. Tonks thought he was doing him a big favour but he wasn't fooled; if he accepted he'd be dragged into a trap, into a world that was hard to escape from once you were enmeshed in it.

'Thanks for bringing me the offer, Barry. Tell your boss – thanks, but I'm not interested.'

Tonks' eyebrows ascended like a bird's wings, descended as a frown. John figured he wasn't at all pleased.

'Mates are important around here, aren't they, kidda?' Tonks said in a sulky voice. 'Know what I mean, like.'

It was John's turn to frown. This was Barry trying to be subtle. What was he implying, exactly?

' 'Course they are,' he said.

'Well, you haven't been acting like they were. You've

been neglecting your mates. People are talking, see.'

John hackles started to rise but he controlled himself, kept his tone even.

'It's still a free country, ain't it? Even in South Bank. I've been busy, Barry.'

Tonks gave him a sly look. 'Busy at the community centre with that big feller, Hooray Henry, or whatever. Even go round his house, I heard.'

'So what?' John shot back at him, bridling. 'He gives me a few boxing lessons, helps me with other things.'

Barry Tonks smiled, but it was a slow, knowing smile, the kind that suggests the possessor has more knowledge than you think he has and he wants you to know it.

'He's been teaching you to read and write. Don't worry, Einstein, we all know.'

That touched a nerve. John felt his face redden, his control slipping.

'I ain't a divvy. I'm just trying to improve.'

It sounded too defensive and weak. Tonks seized on it with the speed of a cat's paw.

'What good is learning to you? Look around you, my old son. There's nowhere to go. Might as well take my man's offer, make some cash instead of beating your brain against a wall – for nowt.'

John felt himself growing more agitated, didn't like the idea that Tonks had found out what was meant to be a secret. He didn't blame Henry though. No doubt one of the lads had overheard a conversation between them, put two and two together and Tonks had learned about it that way.

'I've told you no already, haven't I?'

The gang leader had enough savvy to realize from John's manner that they'd reached a crisis point, that he'd pushed him as far as he would go without an angry confrontation.

'Just thinking of you, John. You're turning down good money, and there ain't any trees for it to grow on around here.'

'You find your tree, Barry, let me find mine.'

Tonks cocked an eyebrow. 'Sounds like a parting of the way, that does.'

John drew in a breath. 'Nothing has changed as far as I'm concerned, except I don't want to deal drugs. My mates are still my mates, but I'm not chained to them – or you.'

They'd reached an impasse. A silence descended. Like strangers with no common ground between them, they stared into each other's eyes, neither willing to look away first. In the distance a police siren screeched like a banshee, broke the spell.

Barry said, gruffly, 'Hooray Henry has enemies. You might have to choose sides.'

'I'll take that as a friendly warning, then.'

'Yeah! Friendly! But if I was you, I'd take the man's offer while you can.'

'No chance, Barry.'

There was little else to say. John was relieved the aggravation hadn't gone further, that his relationship with Tonks hadn't been severed entirely because he had influence over his peers, could make thing difficult for him.

'See you around,' Tonks called over his shoulder. 'When you've got the time.'

John ignored that last jibe, watched him swagger away.

*

Lost in thought, Henry headed for the community centre. Mary's attempt last night to persuade him to give his father a chance to explain things was nagging away at him. She was a sensible woman, Mary, didn't say things without proper consideration. But how could even she understand the true depth of his hurting? You had to stand in another person's shoes to know such things. The sword had penetrated deeper than she knew.

Noticing the police car outside the centre, he increased his stride. There could be a thousand reasons why it was there, he supposed, but he had a sense of foreboding that somehow it had to do with him. He tried to dismiss it as natural fear of the law, the consequence of just leaving prison, but as he walked through the door his presentiment was a stalking shadow at his side.

What he saw brought him up short. For a moment, he felt a sensation in his head, as though an aeroplane was spinning out of control in his brain, roaring a protest as it descended. The reason was that the hall looked as though a bomb had hit it. Broken furniture was strewn about the floor, doors and walls daubed with paint. A smashed computer, wires protruding at crazy angles, had been thrown into the boxing ring. Henry's heart sank at the pure maliciousness of the destruction. That presentiment prodded him again. Was this his brother's handiwork?

Micky was at the back of the hall talking to two policemen. Henry manoeuvred his way between the broken furniture and discarded paint pots. Closer now, he saw the weary, resigned look on Micky's face. His shoulders were drooping uncharacteristically and he seemed shrunken. For once, he looked his age.

When their eyes met, Henry knew instantly they were thinking the same thing; Barry Tonks had delivered a warning, suggesting the place might go up in smoke; this wasn't a fire, but was more than likely a preliminary salvo. As Mick introduced him to the law, he wondered whether he should mention Tonks' threat. Mick pre-empted him.

'I've told these gentlemen we've no idea who could have done this.'

Mick's meaningful stare told him to agree. He knew why; Mick was old school, believed you took care of trouble yourself.

'No idea,' Henry said dolefully.

They answered a few routine questions. One of the policemen said he'd arrange for regular patrols to watch the place, especially at night. Then Henry and Micky saw them off the premises and retreated to the kitchen.

'I'm so sorry, Mick,' Henry said, his voice breaking with emotion. 'I should have gone to the police and told them about Tonks. I'm sure my brother is behind this.' He put his head in his hands. 'You've done me favours and paid a price. I'll have to pack it in here, or something worse will happen.'

Mick pulled Henry's hands away from his face. There was a stubborn set to his jaw, a hard look in his eyes as he looked at the younger man.

'Never told you why I started all this, did I?'

Henry frowned, couldn't see the relevance, muttered, 'You like boxing, like helping the kids around here. Why else?'

Mick dropped his eyes, stared at the floor. Henry sensed he was excavating into his past for something he kept deep down.

'There's more to it than that, son. You see, I wasn't always a straight up guy who lived by the rules.'

Henry forced a smile. 'And here's me thinking you were a vicar's son.'

The trainer's head came up but he didn't respond to Henry's levity, didn't return the smile.

'When I first started to box, I was a wild, cocky kid. One night I had one drink too many and picked on a kid smaller and younger than me over nothing. The kid was brave, stood up to me. The red mist descended.' Micky hesitated, drew his hand across his face. There was real pain in his eyes now. 'I beat the hell out of him, just because I could.'

Henry didn't know what to say. He couldn't imagine Mick as a bully.

'You'd had a drink, didn't know what—'

Micky gave him a dismissive look. 'No excuses! I put him in a coma. He was in it for a few weeks and he came out of it with no side effects, thank God.' Mick drew in a deep breath. 'Those weeks of waiting were the worst of my life.'

Henry could see the old man's pain transcending the years, resurrecting itself in his face.

Struggling for appropriate response, Henry mumbled, 'Must have been a nightmare.'

'Yes! So was the time I served for grievous bodily harm. I was just lucky it wasn't murder.'

Henry was astonished, did his best to hide it. The effort

106

it had been for Micky to talk about it was evident.

'Did you ever box again?' As soon as he'd said it, Henry thought it was a stupid, insensitive question. But the trainer didn't dismiss the question.

'Sure, but I was never the same. I'd lost something, didn't go for it the same way.'

'I can understand that,' Henry said. 'I've been down that road.'

'When I finished boxing, I wanted to put something back. If I'm red hot on discipline it's because I've been lost in that red mist, know what can happen if you let yourself lose control.'

Micky had a faraway look in his eyes as though in his mind he was confronting his younger self. Henry reached out, touched his arm, brought him back.

'You didn't have to tell me all this, Micky. It doesn't make any difference to how—'

Mick gave a faint shake of his head, raised his chin. 'I never quit a student of mine, don't intend to. Second chances are my stock in trade because, believe me, we all need them. Nobody knows that better than me. So don't let me hear any more talk of you quitting. We'll ride this out together.'

His loyalty touched Henry but at the same time worried him. He understood him now better than before, didn't want to see his life's work ruined. The fire Barry Tonks had hinted at might very well be next on the agenda.

'I've got mates, Henry. They'll take a turn at sleeping here to watch the place. With the police patrolling, it'll be OK.'

Henry wasn't as confident. Frank didn't like being

thwarted at anything, especially so when there was money at stake. Mick didn't know him.

He punched Henry lightly on the shoulder. 'Come on, I don't want any argument. Let's start cleaning this place up.'

Henry manufactured a smile. 'Hope you don't regret this.'

'Just you stay off that bare knuckle stuff and I won't.'

They worked for hours cleaning the place up. When evening drew in, they laid off, intending to finish up the next day. Henry left Micky to lock up and set off for home. The walk helped him clear his head and by the time he'd arrived, he'd made a decision. Mary had told him to go and see his father. He'd do that now, reluctantly, because he owed it to Micky to try everything to end this thing before it went to the next level.

It took Henry all the following morning to work himself up to visiting his father; it was near midday as he entered the site. Stretching its chain to its limit, a mongrel barked at him, showed him its not so pearly whites. It set off a cacophony of barking as other dogs took up the refrain. Curtains twitched as he passed along the line of caravans and he knew, though the place seemed deserted, eyes were watching, wondering what his business was here. Unbidden, memories came flooding back from another life, surprised him with their poignancy.

He recognized the caravan from the figure of a boxer painted on the door. As he approached, the sound of a spluttering cough came from inside. He started to have second thoughts, wanted to turn away, avoid this meeting.

What good would it do? Hadn't he vowed never to return?

A minute passed and he was still standing there, anchored to the spot by the weight of old hurts. He decided this was a bad idea. What had he been thinking? For him, the past was not just another country, it was a minefield best avoided. He turned away, ready to abort his mission but the door creaked open and he froze like a thief caught in the act. The voice was so familiar it seemed it was only yesterday he'd heard it last.

'Can't face your old man, eh?'

As though he was dragging his feet through mud, Henry turned around, stepped towards him. His father's features hadn't altered but his face looked drawn and haggard whilst his physique, once so bulky, seemed to have shrunk so that his shoulders were rounded. Thick stubble, once not tolerated as a matter of pride, grew on his chin. Henry couldn't hide his surprise, stood there as self-conscious as a shy schoolboy.

'You've got this far, might as well come on in,' Fred Torrance said.

He made a beckoning gesture and went back inside, accompanied by a coughing bout like the dogs' barks. Bracing himself, Henry followed, tried not to think of anything except that he wasn't here of his own volition but in consideration of other people's welfare.

His father was seated at a table, empty beer bottles arranged around him like a fort. He'd draped a blanket over his shoulders and it made him look like an Indian chief. Henry noticed the kitchen sink was laden with dirty dishes. The place looked like it needed a good clean and, judging by the pervading musty smell, a good airing too.

This was not what he had expected, not how he remembered his old home.

'Sit on those brains of yours,' his father said, showing a flash of that patronizing attitude that was more in keeping with Henry's memories but lacked the same edge of conviction it once had.

Henry slid into the seat opposite, feeling like a child again. He realized he hadn't opened his mouth yet.

His father fixed him with his eyes. Henry couldn't read anything in them.

'Took you long enough to come visit, lad.'

Henry's hackles rose. Five years dismissed in one sentence. The old man had certainly changed outwardly, but his thought processes hadn't altered; he was still selfish to the core.

'You never visited me once inside,' Henry snapped back, his bitterness spilling into his words. 'Not once!'

His old man surprised Henry by having the grace to look embarrassed. It only lasted a moment, though. Then he shrugged his shoulders.

'Had my reasons, son.'

Son! That was an endearment Henry hadn't heard before. Another surprise. He grew suspicious. Had age and weakness forced the old man to adopt new tactics in his dealings because the old bluntness wouldn't work anymore? Was he going to soft soap him to get him to fight Chip Jackson? Well, whatever he tried, it wouldn't work.

'There are no reasons to excuse a father not visiting his son in five years. Shows what you thought of me, doesn't it?'

His father studied the bottles pensively, as though he was trying to find the right words but finding it a struggle.

'Didn't want to see you shut up like an animal,' he said finally, not meeting Henry's gaze. 'Couldn't face it.'

'Poor you!' Henry said, not believing a word of it, yet admitting to himself his father was putting on a good show of sincerity, revealing more emotion than ever he had before.

'Best you were left to get on with it,' Fred continued. 'Seeing me would have reminded you of better days, made things worse. That's what I decided.'

Henry snorted. 'Now I've heard everything! You were thinking of me!'

Silence descended. Henry waited. Any minute his father would mention he'd put money on him fighting, ask him to go up against Chip Jackson. But the old man didn't say anything. He had a guilty look about him. Henry figured it was just good acting. Deciding to push things along, he leaned towards him.

'You've put up a stake for me to take on Chip Jackson. That's right, isn't it?'

Fred covered his face with his hands, drew them slowly down until he was looking at Henry over the tips of his fingers.

'No fool like an old fool, I suppose. I was drunk, son.'

There it was again, that 'son'. As for his father being self critical – that was a new one and no doubt a sly attempt for sympathy.

'Drunk, eh! So what's new under the sun?'

Ignoring the barb, the old man looked straight into Henry's eyes.

111

'Frank tells me you won't fight; is that because it's me asking?'

'Don't flatter yourself,' Henry rasped. 'I've just done five years for killing a Jackson. Now you ask me to risk the same because you've been stupid. When I won't, Frank tries to mess up my life. The only reason I'm here is to ask you to call him off.'

Fred raised his eyebrows in what looked like genuine surprise.

'I didn't know he was at it. Believe me, I didn't. He was just going to talk to you, nothing more.'

Henry took a deep breath. This new soft side the old man was trying to project was a little confusing, not at all what he'd expected. But he didn't trust him.

'Then call him off and prove it.'

His father screwed his face up. 'You think he listens to me anymore? Look at me, son. I'm a sick old man. He does his own thing, your brother. Has done for a long time.'

Henry could see the evidence of his father's decline. That physical presence, which he had relied on to get his way, had waned dramatically. Frank could well have taken advantage.

Suddenly, the old man banged his fist on the table. His eyes sparked the way Henry remembered, as though inside the weaker body his younger self was trying to assert itself, beat the count.

'The Torrances are fighters,' he declaimed. 'Always have been. It's your birthright.'

There it was, out in the open, the attitude Henry had expected when he'd walked in. This was his true self showing through at last. The rest had been a veneer and he'd nearly fallen for it. Now the volcano would erupt and they'd be at each other's throats.

'Like always, you weren't listening to me,' he snapped. 'I tell you I won't fight for anyone. No amount money is enough to make me.'

Henry prepared himself for an angry reaction. If he didn't fight his father would have to hand over the money anyway. Those were the rules the Jacksons played by. One time, nothing could have provoked Fred Torrance more than that. Yet, the volcano didn't show any sign of blowing. Instead his father seemed to shrink right into himself, looked defeated. When he spoke all the passion that had resurged a moment ago was gone.

'I can see you've made up your mind. Can't say I blame you either. I was never much of a father, especially after your mother died.' He gave a long sigh that made his chest rattle. 'I can't make any claims on you, Henry. You do what you think you have to.'

As though being too close to the old man might give him a wrong perspective, Henry leaned away from him. He was confused. He couldn't see any sign that he was acting; there was more acceptance than artifice in his eyes.

'You can at least tell Frank to stop.'

'I'll try, but he won't listen.' Fred hesitated, cocked an eyebrow at him. 'You're sure you won't fight? All that talent of yours going to waste – those preening Jacksons needing to be brought down a peg.'

His father's tone had been more wistful than anything, without any true conviction or aggressiveness. Henry couldn't get angry.

'Not to mention your money is involved, eh? The truth

is I'm ashamed of my past. I want to better myself in other ways.'

When the old man didn't answer, Henry stood up and started for the door. As he'd expected, his visit had been fruitless. He thought his father would call him back, make one final appeal to get him to fight, but the only sound when he opened the door was a dog howling at some perceived injustice.

Hand on the door handle, he turned. His father was watching him from behind the bottle fort, looking lonely and melancholy, like the last survivor of a battle who feels guilty he hasn't gone down with his comrades. In spite of himself, Henry felt a pang of sympathy. He heard himself speak in a voice that was so dry it didn't seem his own.

'You stand to lose all your savings?'

His father nodded. 'Yeah! More fool me. But I'll still have my caravan so I'll get by – always have.'

Henry grunted. A feeling of regret swept over him. He wished things could have been different between his father and him, but too much had happened, or not happened. As he started to step out, his father called after him.

'Good luck with your life, Henry. You never had much going for you. I should have done better by you.'

Henry looked back, perplexed. Was his father genuine or just a wily old fox fighting with the tricks it had left? Strangely, he thought he was being sincere. Again, he couldn't find words. The lump rising in his throat didn't help and he settled for a nod in his father's direction. As he shut the door behind him it felt like closing a book with a nagging sense of dissatisfaction because it had raised questions which would remain unanswered unless he dipped into it again.

As he headed off the site, he knew he hadn't solved anything coming here. He believed his old man when he said he couldn't control his brother. You just had to look at him to know he was incapable of imposing his rule. He'd accepted his refusal to fight without much of an argument. The biggest surprise, however, the one that had set Henry's emotions swirling, were those final, humble, apologetic good wishes. That was something he hadn't expected in a million years. And he'd called him son – twice.

John Walsh felt happier than he had for a long time. In the past fortnight, he'd had three visits to the Fairbrother farm to help Henry with the horses, enjoying the animals and the natural surroundings, the sense it gave him that there were other horizons beyond South Bank. The chestnut welcomed him like an old friend each time and the other horses were gradually losing their fear. It was a good feeling, that trust which was developing, the giving and receiving of affection with no sense of ulterior motive. The fact that Tonks and his pals knew he was trying to educate himself didn't concern him the way it had before, seemed a triviality.

He'd just come into the house. Henry had set him some homework and, since the place seemed quiet, he decided to take advantage, head straight upstairs to his bedroom and get on with it. Usually his books were in the bedside cabinet so he was puzzled when he couldn't find them. Thinking he could have left them under the bed, he searched there but with no result. Now he started to panic. Had his father been in his room ? Aware of noises coming from the garden, he moved to the window to investigate.

A fire was blazing out there. His father and two of his wastrel mates were perched beside it, using beer crates for seats. A barbecue grill lay across the fire. As though a sixth sense had told him his son was watching, his father glanced up at the bedroom window, locked eyes with his son. John could have sworn he saw a smile on his lips as he reached down. The next instant his father was holding a book in his hands. With slow deliberation, as though relishing it, he tore out the pages, fed them to the flames.

John watched in disbelief, his emotions swirling. Then those emotions condensed to a white hot fury that impelled him out of the bedroom. He galloped down the stairs, burst out of the door. Heart pounding, he stood before his father and his pals who were grinning at him inanely. Two books lay at his father's feet. John stooped, picked them up as though they were precious gold, held them to his chest. Glancing at the fire, he saw the last vestiges of his other books consumed in the flames.

John fought hard for self-control but bitter resentment stoked his anger. There was no doubt in his mind his father had done this deliberately. He was jealous, didn't want him to better himself, was afraid his son might do better than him, be something he couldn't be. How else could you explain his actions?

'We're not to be disturbed, Shakespeare. Can't yer see we're dining?' his old man slurred. He bit into a bun, tomato sauce squelching out like blood from a wound.

'Hark at Lord Charlie! He's dining out tonight,' one of the men cackled, nearly falling off his crate in the process.

'Pass the port, Charlie,' the other fellow slurred in what

116

was meant to be a posh voice but fell way short.

His father laughed with them, then looked at John with bleary eyes that had no merriment, only a slyness that conveyed to his son he knew exactly what he had done and didn't give a damn.

'We're having a ceremony,' he said. 'It's called the burning of the books. Hitler had one. What was good enough for Hitler—'

John could no longer contain his fury. He swung his right boot and sent the grill flying. Pieces of meat shot through the air, landed on the grass.

A silence heavy with implication descended on the group. His father's pals stared at the meat sizzling in the grass as though entranced.

'Yer little bastard,' his father said, when he'd recovered from the shock. 'That's our grub.'

John clutched his remaining books to his chest. 'You couldn't just let me be, could you?' he yelled. 'You had to try to keep me down, like always. Hitler? Hitler had nothing on you.'

His father rose, took a step towards his son, his face contorted.

'And who do you think you are?' he sneered, spittle shooting from his mouth. 'You never did nowt at school and now you waste your time with them . . . things. Get a job if anybody'll have a useless article like you. Make some money. Yer mother spoiled yer, put ideas into that stupid head. That's what's wrong with you.'

'You tell him, Charlie!' one of the men called out, clapping his hands.

The injustice of his father's words rekindled John's fury.

117

He knew it would be best to walk away as he usually did, but this time he couldn't.

'My mother was too good for you,' he shouted. 'She should have left you. She was the one who worked while you sat on your fat backside. You and your mates are one of a kind – ignorant wasters – kings of the slag heaps. I'd rather die than end up like you.'

Charlie Walsh's face was incandescent. His son was hammering him right into the ground and insulting his mates for good measure. It was too much for him to bear. Drawing back his arm, he swung a punch at John's head. The movement was so ponderous he saw it coming, easily avoided the blow. On another day John might have let it go, but he was already furious. Now the red mist came down. He struck his father hard in the stomach. Charlie Walsh bent double, let out a groan, followed it with a volley of spew which landed in his mate's lap. Sinking down on one knee like a holy man seeking a blessing, he looked up at his son but with nothing remotely holy in his eyes, only hatred.

John felt guilty, yet strangely elated, all at once. It was time to make a retreat so he ran to the back gate, burst out into the back alley. He told himself he'd given his old man what he deserved, what he'd had coming for a long time. Yet he couldn't shake off a sense of shame, because for a moment back there he'd totally lost it, had wanted to tear his old man to pieces. He'd been in another dimension where nothing mattered but doing some damage. He felt he'd let Henry down.

An old instinct drove him through the streets and across the disused railway track to the abandoned pigeon lofts where his grandfather had once kept his birds. The lofts had long since been damaged by vandals, but his grandfather's old loft still had half a roof, would give a bit of shelter and a place to think. He crawled through a hole in the wire, entered the ramshackle hut and lay down on the wooden floor.

As he lay there listening to his own laboured breathing, a myriad thoughts raced through his head. There was no doubt what he had just done had changed everything, had tilted the axis of his world. With that punch, the balance of power had shifted and his old man would know it. Charlie Walsh carried grudges, was an unforgiving man, even if John wanted to be forgiven, which he didn't. He couldn't face living in that house with his father any longer. It would crush the life and hope out of him just when he'd started to believe. But where could he go? With no money how would he survive?

It was early morning. On the lonely streets the rain was starting to fall, at first softly, like a baby's tears, then gathering force, as though the gods needed to remind John Walsh he was at the mercy of the power of nature and it could turn on him at a whim. Stiff and miserable from a night spent in the pigeon loft, he took shelter in a shop doorway, wiped the rain from his face and hair and looked out at the wet streets of South Bank feeling like an animal without a lair to give it protection against the elements. Had he now officially joined the ranks of the homeless?

He half turned, realized it was a butcher's shop. So near he felt he could almost reach out and touch them, a smug looking plethora of pork pies sat in the window like squat,

119

brown-skinned men in competition to see who had the best tone and tan. The vision set his digestive juices on the rampage. His stomach growled its discontent. It had been twelve hours since he'd eaten. Never mind a roof over his head, where would his next meal come from? Perhaps he'd watch the house, wait for his father to go out, then slip back in and help himself. Not a long term solution, not an easy manoeuvre, but a necessary one.

His eye on the pies, he took no particular notice when a Ford Fiesta drew up at the kerb. He heard his name called. When he looked, the driver's window was down and Barry Tonks was staring at him through the relentless sheets of rain.

'Not going to rob that shop, are you, John?'

'Just eyeing those pork pies,' he answered, jerking a thumb at the window, trying valiantly to sound light-hearted.

Tonks raised his eyes to the sky, beckoned with his hand.

'Ha'way man, get yourself out of the wet for a minute.'

John hesitated. Tonks seemed to have dismissed the edginess between them at their last meeting. He knew he didn't have a licence and the car was likely stolen – or borrowed. But he was cold and miserable and right now any port in a storm was better than none. The warm car was tempting so he ran round to the passenger side and climbed in.

'You look like death warmed up – maybe not as good as that,' Tonks said, eyeing John as he settled into the seat. 'What's up with you, feller?'

Tonks wasn't the ideal agony aunt, far from it, but John felt like unburdening himself.

'Fell out with my old man big time, didn't I? Don't think I can go back home.'

Tonks' eyes fixed on his like two laser guns locked on a target.

'You'll need a bit of cash, then?'

John shook his head. He had an idea what might be coming next, didn't want to know.

'Forget it, Barry. I ain't going to deal drugs.'

'Naw, man, you got me wrong. I just want someone to drive me somewhere, then back again. Got to make a special delivery, see.'

'So this special delivery has nothing to do with drugs and you're incapable of driving yourself there. Pull the other one, Barry.'

'It's nowt to do with drugs,' Tonks protested. 'It's a fair distance and you know I'm a bad driver. You were always better than me when we nicked cars.'

That much was true. John didn't like being reminded, but when they were fourteen they'd stolen cars a couple of times, gone joy riding. Luckily they'd not been caught in spite of Barry's erratic driving.

'Twenty quid for just driving and minding the car.' Tonks said. 'As Mr Tarrant says, "final offer".'

At that moment, twenty quid seemed a fortune. John was tempted. He figured it would help him to eat for a few days while he tried to sort out his next move.

'I just drive, that's all? There's nothing criminal going on?'

'Naw, man. I swear it. Just a little job.'

John stared out of the windscreen. A scrawny pigeon waddled into a puddle on the pavement to peck at a discarded pizza. He could empathize with the creature. It seemed like a brother in need.

'All right then, I'll do it,' he said, noticing the butcher was about to open the shop. 'For twenty quid – and a pork pie from the shop.'

'Deal,' Tonks said, looking pleased with himself.

They both got out of the car. John slid into the driver's seat while Tonks entered the shop. When he returned, he sat in the passenger's seat and handed John a pork pie which was consumed with relish.

'We're going for a nice drive in the country,' Tonks told him.

John set off, followed the roads Tonks had written down on a piece of paper and soon they were on the outskirts of Middlesbrough with the Cleveland Hills in view. He recognized the roads because they were the same ones they'd used on their way to Peter Fairbrother's farm.

When they arrived at Great Ayton, he began to wonder at the coincidence but then they took a road he hadn't been down before and he figured coincidence was all it could be. Eventually, Tonks directed him off the main road, down a single track lane overarched with trees. Thick bushes grew profusely between the trees making it difficult to see anything beyond the lane's confines. Tonks told him to stop the car.

'Just wait here,' he told John. 'I'll be back in ten minutes, max.'

He was out of the car before John had a chance to speak. Through the mirror, he watched him remove something from the boot and stuff it inside his jacket but couldn't see what it was. In the blink of an eye, he disappeared through the bushes.

Now that he was alone, John had time to think. In normal circumstances, he wouldn't have had anything to do with any of Barry Tonks' enterprises. Tonks wasn't above lying, could be conducting a drug deal right now for all he knew. After five minutes, his curiosity got the better of him. He got out of the car, paced restlessly, then scrambled through the bushes.

When he emerged on the other side, he realized he was at the edge of the field where Peter Fairbrother kept the horses. The house was a quarter mile off to his right, the barn in a straight line 200 yards away. John's stomach started to churn. This was stretching coincidence beyond its limit. What was Tonks up to? Did he know he worked with those horses?

He scanned the ground, spotted a figure lying in the grass near the barn. Tonks! He watched the gang leader rise to his feet. Something flared in his hand. A torch? He started towards the barn. John couldn't believe the evidence of his own eyes. Was this a bad dream? Surely he wasn't going to torch the stables? His body felt numb, as though an invisible force was pressing in on him, weighing him down. He started to panic, searched the field for the horses, couldn't see them, realized they must be inside. Tonks was slipping through the door and still he was rooted to the spot like a soldier with battle shock, paralysed by the horror of what he was witnessing.

His body was still in a state of inertia, his brain refusing to give it orders as, seconds later, Tonks burst out the barn, closed the doors and started to run. A lazy curl of smoke escaped under the doors, shaped itself into a cloud. That left no room for any more doubt in John's mind. Revivified, he leapt the fence. Visions of those horses he'd come to love flashed into his mind as he covered the ground. He imagined their flesh burning, their agonized screams. It drove him on faster.

Tonks saw him coming, broke his stride, veered into his path, arms splayed to halt his progress.

'What the hell are you doing?' he yelled. 'Get back!'

John had an urge to batter him to the ground but had other priorities. He knocked him out of the way, focused his eyes on the stables, remembering how the old chestnut nuzzled him, trusted him even when one of his kind had already given it such a good reason to hate all men. He threw himself at the doors with all his strength. They yielded easily to his ferocity.

Inside, the flames had taken hold, were eating ravenously, red tongues competing in an orgy of gluttony. Like a sly accomplice, the smoke crept around them obscuring John's vision so that he could only just make out the stalls. Frightened whinnying cut right to his heart. He could hear hoofs pounding on wood. Coughing and spluttering, he rushed through the flames, ignoring the waves of heat that slapped against his face. He opened the first two stalls and stepped aside. Slipping and sliding in their panic, the horses rushed out, became more sure footed as they ran for the stable doors.

The third stall was the chestnut's. He saw instantly it was in a worse state than the others, its eyes wide and rolling, its great chest heaving as it fought for breath. Tears in his eyes, not just from smoke, John grabbed a bridle. His presence and his voice calmed it enough for him to slip the bridle on. Talking to it with a calmness he did not feel, he led it out of the stall, through the smoke and flames to the door and into the fresh air.

John released the bridle and the chestnut limped away. He doubled up, gasping for breath. He wanted to go after the chestnut but didn't have time. Down at the farmhouse, he could see a blonde head sticking out of one of the windows. Peter Fairbrother's wife! At that distance, he doubted she'd recognize him but any moment she'd be sounding the alarm and all hell would break loose. Self-preservation kicked in. He started to run, didn't turn to look back until he reached the fence. He saw men running towards the stables which were shrouded in smoke. With a final glance at the corner of the field where the three horses had gathered, he hurled himself over the fence.

There was no sign of the car and he didn't have time to lament the fact. If anyone had spotted him, they would be coming after him. With too little time to form a plan, he took off down the lane towards the main road, cursing Tonks, himself too for trusting him when he should have known better.

Running at full tilt, he rounded a bend and came up short. There was a car ahead, two men leaning on the bonnet. He scrambled into the bushes, grateful the men were facing another way, hadn't seen him. Were they part of a search party? Surely, there hadn't been time to organize one? Either way, he couldn't risk being seen, was trapped, the clock ticking against him.

Suddenly a third man stepped out of the tree-line. At a signal from him all three pulled balaclavas over their heads and jumped into the car. The engine roared and it took off, dirt squirting under the back tyres. John breathed a sigh of relief. Whatever those men were doing, their business didn't involve him. He started running, reached the main road, crossed over, leapt a fence into a field, ran alongside a hedge for cover.

When he'd put distance between himself and the stables, he rested for a moment, allowed his breathing to settle down. Tonks was in his mind, as painfully as a needle sticking in his flesh. There was no excusing what the gang leader had done. He hated him for it. Did he have ice in his veins instead of blood? That he'd been there to save the horses was the one blessing out of the whole mess. If he hadn't been there, he dreaded to think of their fate.

Now he had the problem of getting home and he decided to walk, keeping off the main roads because the police would be watching them. When he was clear of the area he would try to catch a bus in one of the small villages. As he set off again, he was already dreading having to tell Henry Torrance what had happened. However badly it reflected on himself, he knew he had to tell him the truth.

It was dark when Henry heard the knock on his door. He wasn't used to late night visitors so he opened up cautiously, peered out. It took a moment before his eyes adjusted and he could recognize the tired, bedraggled figure on the doorstep. Even in the poor light, he could see the strain in John Walsh's face, his embarrassment as he shifted his weight from one foot to the other like an agitated parrot on a perch. John's mouth opened but nothing came out. He tried again with the same result. Finding words seemed a step too far for him and it didn't take genius on Henry's part to gather something must be very wrong in John Walsh's life.

'What's happened to you,' Henry said gently.

John found his voice, stammered, 'I've left home and I'm living in a pigeon loft.'

'You look like you need some food inside you, son.' Henry beckoned him to follow him inside. 'I've just been to the chippy. You're welcome to share my fish and chips.'

When John was seated in the lounge, Henry retreated to the kitchen, emerged with two plates of fish and chips, a pot of tea and a copious amount of buttered bread, all laid out on a tray. John attacked his food with such indecent haste Henry knew he couldn't have eaten much that day, remained silent while his visitor demolished the food right down to the last crumb. Replete at last, John shot his host an embarrassed glance.

'Want to talk about what happened?'

John couldn't meet Henry's eye. He stared down at the carpet as though its patterns were gateways into another world where he would rather be than in the real one around him. The clock on the mantelpiece ticked off each second of their impasse but Henry didn't press him. Finally, John raised his head, looked straight at Henry, gave a resigned sigh and told him everything that had happened to him from the moment he'd found his books missing.

Henry listened without interrupting, his emotions vacillating between sympathy for John Walsh, undisguised horror when he heard about the fire, fury at Tonks' callous actions. When he'd finished, John buried his head in his hands.

'I've let you down,' he mumbled through his fingers, 'I was an idiot to take notice of Tonks. Should have known no good would come of it.'

Henry's brain was reeling. He was sure burning his place of work was Tonks' way of getting back at him. He had his suspicions about the men John had seen in the lane but kept silent about that for now, focused on John. There was no doubting the lad had been foolish, but in his circumstances how many could say they wouldn't have done the same?

'Go easy on yourself,' he said. 'You made a bad mistake but I'm proud of the way you went in to save the horses. You could have just panicked, run off and left them to die. You passed the real test.'

John removed his hands from his face. There were tracks on his cheeks where the tears had run down.

'You really think so?'

'I know so.'

That seemed to cheer him up. His voice was stronger.

'You don't think it was all a coincidence?'

'No more than I think South Bank is a tourist trap.'

'Tonks was getting back at you. That's what you think?'

'It certainly looks that way.'

'Those men in balaclavas,' John mused. 'Do you think they were going to the farmhouse.'

Henry frowned. 'The fire could have been a distraction to get the people out in the field.'

John focused on Henry with greater intensity.

'You mean they used Tonks.'

Henry was pretty sure he knew the answer but didn't want John to know how worried he was.

'You're weaving a web there, Inspector Morse. I'm due up there tomorrow so I'll find out if the place was robbed – or if anything worse happened. Probably you shouldn't come with me until I see how the land lies.'

John took on a pained expression. 'I hope we're wrong – maybe they were poachers or something.'

'Did you get a good look at any of them?'

John shook his head. 'Didn't really get close – but there was one thing.'

'Go on.'

'The one that came out of the trees. Now I think about it he was something like you, something about his face, the way he moved.'

Henry smiled ruefully. John was helping confirm his underlying suspicion. It wouldn't be the first time Frank had been likened to him and vice versa.

John caught the smile. 'Do you know those men?'

The lad was sharp. Henry had to give him that. He'd shown considerable trust coming to him and confessing. Perhaps it was time to do some confessing of his own. Taking a deep breath, he plunged in.

'If I tell you something about myself, something that I did that was wrong, can you keep it to yourself?'

John didn't hesitate. 'You've tried to help me, been a real mate. Goes without saying, doesn't it?'

Henry began his tale. No matter what he was thinking, John showed no emotion as he told him about his prison sentence, his relationship with his father and brother, how his brother was trying to force him into the fight.

'So you can see what's going down,' Henry concluded. 'I've no intention of fighting and Frank's trying to pressure

129

me. I'm almost certain it was him you saw, that he was using Barry Tonks.'

'You could call the police anonymously,' John suggested. 'Tell them you think your brother was behind the fire.'

'My brother's too clever to leave evidence. Besides, this is gypsy business we're talking about. Gypsies don't grass. That's the way I was brought up.'

'You're in as big a mess as me,' John said. 'And your father sounds like mine – no use to man nor beast.'

'The last time I saw mine,' Henry said, 'he'd changed. It took me by surprise that he'd mellowed.'

'Mine won't,' John said. 'He's set in stone.'

Henry felt for the lad. He knew from bitter experience what it was like to have nobody to turn to in your hour of need. It was so easy to stray when you had nobody you respected to take an interest and guide you.

'If you want to you can bed down in my spare room until things calm down.'

John's face lit up. 'That's good of you, if you're sure—'

'I'm sure. Bed's all made up. You look as though you need sleep right now so go on up. It's the first on the right.'

John didn't need any more encouragement. After his exhausting day, he was fighting to stay awake. Henry was left alone in the lounge and his thoughts were bleak. The worst thought of all was how close the horses had come to been burned alive. It was unbelievable that a brother of his could be involved in that. He could only hope there wouldn't be worse news tomorrow.

Frank Torrance pulled his car onto the concrete space, glanced across at his father's caravan. It was late and he was tired after a busy day. He hoped the old man hadn't heard him arrive. He couldn't face it if he came shambling over to keep him up with small talk. Time the old guy croaked it, no doubt about that; he'd gone downhill and then some in the last year. Hard to imagine now the times when he'd been afraid of him. These days he had no respect for him. If ever he became so useless, Frank hoped someone would give him a pill, put him out of his misery.

Thinking of uselessness brought to mind the raid on the Fairbrother place earlier. The safe had been right up to date and unyielding. All they'd managed to spirit away were two paintings from the walls, which he figured might bring a thousand, tops. Divided three ways it was a paltry reward. The main point though, the whole object of the operation, was that Henry could be in no doubt he was right into his life, biting at his tail until he agreed to fight Chip Jackson. The trouble was his brother could be a stubborn cuss like himself, like their father had been in his pomp. The Jacksons weren't paragons of patience. Henry had to fight or there was no way out for Frank except in a coffin.

Frank felt a shiver run up his spine. The Jacksons walking over his grave? If the fire didn't emphasize to Henry how far beyond serious he was, he'd have to crank up the pressure, maybe kidnap the girlfriend, hold her somewhere until it was done and dusted.

He was surprised that the door was already ajar, had a moment of trepidation, thinking perhaps he'd been burgled, the biter bitten. Then he remembered his old man had a key that fitted, was in the habit of borrowing things when he wasn't there. He must have come over earlier, forgotten to lock the door after him, another sign of his failing faculties. Tomorrow he'd have to remember to ask for the key back. He felt for the light switch but decided the old man might notice the light on, head over when all he wanted to do was get to bed, not get drunk with him, waste his time listening to maudlin reminiscences.

He slipped his jacket off in the dark, started to undress, had just got one leg out of his trousers, was balancing precariously when the whole place lit up. Losing his balance, he fell against the cooker, set off a discordant rattling as pans jumped and clashed, nagging at his already frayed nerves. Then he saw them and his nerves climbed to the top of the scale, from nagging to screaming.

Three men were in the caravan, two of them seated on the couch, the other standing with one hand on the light switch. Bizarrely, just for a second he thought they were ghosts. But he soon realized they were far from other worldly, that it wasn't spirits but the Jacksons in the flesh who'd invaded his home. Fear, and an awareness his state of undress must make him look ludicrous to these hard men, caused the blood to rush to his face.

'One leg in, one leg out – shake it all about,' Danny Jackson said, smirking at Jet, who was the one standing. 'That's just you these days, ain't it? Halfway to nowhere, about to trip yourself up and take a big, big fall.'

Frank hauled his trousers back on, regretting he'd ever allowed himself to get into a position where these buffoons could lord it over him as though they were God almighty. He tried to regain his composure. But he knew this was serious. The men were no longer smirking. They were stone faced, like a jury before a pronouncement.

'What are you doing in my home?'

It was an attempt to assert himself, but a poor one. Even to him, his voice sounded like a high pitched travesty, more of a whine really, the question a superfluous inanity because they all knew the answer. He had no room to play the big man.

'You've been out of touch,' Jet said. 'We began to wonder if you'd forgotten us.'

His smile as scornful as his tone, Terry said, 'And the clock's been ticking away – tick tock – tick tock.'

'Your brother,' Danny said, his eyebrows raised. 'He's ready, isn't he?'

Frank flushed to a deeper shade. He was on the hot spot here. Even if he could invent something to give him more time, if they found out he was prevaricating there'd be a price to pay. Best then to tell the truth, hope it would do for now.

'My brother says he won't fight, but I've been working on him – messing with his life. He'll come round in the end.'

The older Jackson stared at him. His eyes seemed to penetrate all the layers of his skin so that there was no artifice which would withstand their scrutiny. He was glad he'd told the truth.

'You got five days,' Danny growled. 'Chip can't hang around waiting for him no matter how bad we want it. There's plenty queuing to fight him. Five days exactly, then we'll want our money.'

Frank felt pain his stomach, as though a wild creature was feeding on him from the inside. He knew the creature's name was fear, could feel its claws scratching at his throat as he answered.

'Didn't think he was going to be so stubborn.' He tried to force the creature back down. 'Can't you make it longer?'

Danny glowered. 'We gave you the money to buy drugs from that Jamaican gang you talked up, said you could trust. Wasn't our fault they took you for a fool. Only an amateur would let himself be robbed of the drugs half an hour after the handover – and by the same gang.'

Laid out bare like that there was nothing he could say. He'd messed up big time and there was no denying it. No excuse in the world would serve.

'You were at it, weren't you?' Jet said. 'You didn't know enough about those fellers, pretended you did and chanced your arm.'

'And with our money,' Terry chipped in with his pennyworth. 'Probably thinking to make yourself a profit and to move into the big time. A man's reach should never outstrip his brains and you got extra short arms.'

Like a teacher manifesting his disappointment in an erring pupil, Danny waggled a finger at Frank.

'You'd be one dead gypsy if you hadn't offered to fix up this fight. With Chip winning and cleaning up on the side bets, we'd get our money back. Even then, we'd likely come up short. But it would be worth a little loss.'

Terry examined his fingernails. 'It was the only chance you had to make it up to us.'

Frank blanched. He didn't like Terry's use of the past tense there. It felt as though he'd already been judged and condemned.

Danny shrugged. 'Otherwise. . . .'

He didn't need to finish. Frank was well aware of the implications. He dragged in a breath, forced out his words.

'Come on, lads. We never set no deadline, did we? He's not long out of jail. He'll come around.'

Jet giggled. Mystified, his father and brother looked at him. He covered his mouth.

'What's so funny, bro'?' Terry said.

Jet managed to control himself. 'Deadline!' he said. 'Dead is how he's gonna be and line is what he's dangling on. That's funny.'

Po-faced, Terry shook his head. 'Yeah, sure. It kills me.'

Jet pointed at Frank, giggled again. 'It's gonna kill him too. I think—'

Danny sliced the air with his hand and his son shut up.

'Take it there's a . . . deadline . . . set now, Frank. Five days' time at Bolt farm near Staithes. Keep that quiet. Just you and us to know.'

Five days, not even a week. It was no time at all. Frank opened his mouth, shut it again. That fear was still crawling around inside him. His brain raced in search of a solution that would extricate him from this nightmare. Snatching the girl, holding her until after Henry fought, might do it. Kidnapping was heavy stuff and he didn't like it one bit, but when your life was on the line—

Danny started for the door and his sons followed him. On the threshold, he paused, reached towards a bowl of fruit, plucked out an apple and pocketed it.

'Ring me,' he said. 'We'll finalize timings. There'll be a big crowd and we don't want things messing up.'

'Yeah!' Terry said with a wicked grin. ' 'Cos messing up is your thing, Frank, ain't it?'

Not to be outdone by his brother, Jet feigned seriousness and said, 'Get a good sleep, Frank. Sometimes dreams are better than real life.'

When they were gone Frank turned the light off, didn't bother undressing, just flopped down on the bed as though his limbs had lost all volition. For a long time he stared into the dark, seeing nothing but blackness, wondered if that was all he had to look forward to if he couldn't bring Henry round to his way of thinking.

Fred Torrance, chest wheezing as he struggled for breath, peeked through the curtains, watched three shadowy figures traverse the ground that only moments ago he'd fled across as fast as his weak limbs had allowed. One arm trailing along the wall for support, he edged towards his chair, sank into it as though he wished the cushions could absorb him entirely and he'd never have to rise out of it to face the world again. But his need for a drink overcame his inertia, motivated him enough to stretch for the whisky bottle on the table. Only when he'd taken two long slugs did he allow himself to ponder what he'd heard, to contemplate the shame of it.

When he'd heard Frank return, he'd gone across to try to persuade him to lay off Henry, accept his refusal. He'd been prepared to hand £40,000 to the Jacksons, as honour demanded, to put an end to the matter his own foolishness had set in motion. He'd heard familiar voices coming from inside the caravan, paused by the open window to listen. The confrontation, if such a one-sided affair could be called that, shocked him to the core of his being. He'd felt old, weak and defeated, as though all his past sins had formed an alliance to attack him, take revenge when he was at his weakest.

His eldest son was using him, playing him for a fool. Equally shaming, he was involved in drug dealing. Fred hadn't been above breaking the law himself in what he considered petty ways, but those who made money from drugs he considered the lowest scum on earth, devoid of humanity. How could he have spawned a son like that? Why hadn't he seen this coming when he already had all the evidence he needed that Frank had a cold heart incapable of feeling?

Anger driving him, he rose, intending to confront his son. But he felt exhausted, sank down, defeated by his own body. How long was he for this earth, he wondered? Two years ago a doctor had told him his heart was weakening, but he hadn't taken much notice. Did he want to go on in his current condition, at the mercy of all and sundry?

He saw now, when it was too late, that all he'd really ever had in the world of true importance were his sons. They would be his only legacy, all that would be left of him. One of them, he'd alienated, while the other had turned rotten, broken ancient bonds a long time ago. Blood turning against blood was unnatural. He should have spoken out, brought the truth into the light.

He didn't want to hear it but the voice of his own conscience persisted, asking how much was down to his failure as a father. When his wife died he'd gone off the rails, thought too much about himself, not enough about the boys. His worst mistake? The secret he'd guarded so long thinking it was for the best.

Wearied by morose thoughts, he started to reach for the bottle but stayed his hand. He'd need to keep a clear head,

137

because he was resolved to see Henry tomorrow, tell him everything he'd heard tonight. It wouldn't make up for the wrong he'd done him, wouldn't lift the albatross from his shoulders. But it was the least he could do to try to make amends.

Henry rose bright and early, looked in on John in the spare bedroom before he came downstairs. The kid was fast asleep, exhausted after his recent trials. He decided he'd take him with him today when he went to see Micky Lane. The prospect wasn't something Henry relished. Micky had taken a chance on him. Now he had to tell him his good deed had turned sour. Peter Fairbrother, who'd been generous and trusting, hadn't deserved what had happened either. What kind of a world was it where bad things happened to good people, where the winds of fate could change direction at a whim. He gave himself a shake. This wasn't a time for philosophizing. You had to be practical. Micky, in his wise way, might come up with something.

Henry looked out. The street was quiet, curtains still drawn. Over the rooftops, the horizon blushed pale red, like the flush on a young girl's cheeks. He was about to turn away when he noticed a taxi coming up the street. Brakes squealed as it pulled to a halt outside his window. At first Henry didn't recognize the hunched figure leaning on a stick for support. It took two takes before he realized it was his father climbing out of the taxi. He was shocked at his decline even in the short time since he'd last seen him. Knowing the way he was, the fact he'd succumbed to a stick was like a last surrender.

138

The bell rang. Poker-faced, Henry opened up. There was no spark in his father's eyes, just a dull, melancholy appeal, the eyes of a beggar hungry in spirit. He'd lost so much weight his anorak swamped him so that he seemed to have no neck. Henry was thrown. He wanted to hate him but he looked so broken and old he found it hard. Confused, he settled for just staring at him, as though he had no business to come to his door.

'I know how you feel about me,' his father said. 'The taxi's coming back in twenty minutes. But I've something important to say, something you have to hear for your own good – not mine.'

Henry nodded. He could stand twenty minutes. His father waved his stick at the taxi and it drove off. He followed his son inside to the lounge. Henry pointed to a chair. His father sat upright in it, leaning on his stick.

'I'm going out soon,' Henry said, frowning to let his father know he was there under sufferance.

Fred took the hint, came straight to the point. 'I understand that I'm not welcome. But you need to know about your brother. That's the only reason I'm here.'

Henry grinned cynically. 'Don't think you can expand my knowledge much. I told you what he was up to and whatever you said to him, if you bothered at all, hasn't stopped him.'

Fred gripped the stick tighter. 'I know why he's forcing it,' he said. His bottom lip trembled and he shook his head in exasperation. 'It's disgusting—.'

Henry glanced ostentatiously at his watch. Whatever his father was going to reveal couldn't add much to the sins Frank had already committed against him.

139

'Like I told you, I'm going out.'

Fred nodded, began talking, poured out everything he heard outside Frank's caravan. His voice shook with emotion as he spoke and his hands trembled. Henry listened, even greater disgust for his brother welling up inside him.

'He's a drug dealer in trouble, using us to help him get off the hook,' Fred concluded, momentarily resting his head on the gnarled fists grasping the stick. When he raised his head again, he looked straight at Henry. 'I wanted you to fight for the right reasons, honourable ones, not to satisfy a bunch of dirty drug dealers. Now I wouldn't want you to fight.'

Henry's eyes locked on his father's. He could see there was no artifice in the old man, that he was genuine.

Henry shook his head. 'They obviously want this fight badly.'

'Don't give them it!' his father said vehemently. He pushed himself up, stood with a blank look. The storm that had raged inside him as he'd told his tale had subsided but left him with a mystified expression.

Henry rose, faced him. 'Are you going to give him your money?'

Fred thrust out his jaw. 'Frank's a dead man walking. I'll give him the money because he's still my son and it was me who shook on it. That's binding even with scum. I won't tell him what I know. He can go his own way.'

Henry couldn't help feeling a pang of sympathy for his father. No way he'd been a good parent and not visiting him in prison had been the last straw, but he had to admit he did seem different.

Henry walked behind him to the door. He was tongue tied, couldn't think of a word to say, those old hurts a barrier. The taxi looming into view rescued him. Fred turned to him, fighting back tears.

'There's something I wish I could tell you,' he muttered, lowering his head like a guilty child.

'Wasn't that enough for one day?'

Fred raised his head as the taxi drew up. The driver opened the door. For a moment the old man stood there not moving. The driver looked bemused by his hesitation and the void of silence exaggerated the noise of the taxi's engine ticking over. Finally Fred emerged from wherever his thoughts had taken him, shuffled towards the vehicle, calling over his shoulder.

'Just can't tell you, Henry. Just can't!'

He bundled himself into the seat, didn't look back as the taxi took off, just stared fixedly ahead. It was as though out there in the ether he could see his future being played out, didn't like it.

Henry retreated inside more than a little confused. His father's revelations hadn't exactly shaken his world, given what his brother had already done to him. The fact that, in his poor physical state, he'd bothered to come to tell him and was set against him fighting, had surprised him though. He'd never seen his old man so emotional and, if he wasn't mistaken, apparently concerned for his welfare. To top it all, there were those last words, spoken with so much regret. What was it, he wondered, that his father found it so difficult to tell him?

Henry wasn't given time to dwell on those matters. As soon as he closed the door the phone rang. It was Father

141

Andrew apologizing for not being in touch sooner, asking how he was coping. He toyed with the idea of telling him he was in trouble but thought better of it. Being the man he was, the priest would want to help him and it was way out of his league. Knowing his fearless streak, he might blunder into a situation where his dog collar would mean nothing to those who'd made a pact with the Devil.

Trying to sound cheerful, he said, 'I'm doing OK, thanks.'

'Good lad.'

The priest hesitated and Henry wondered what was coming next.

'There's a favour you could do for me, son.'

'Of course. You've done me plenty.' Henry forced a laugh. 'Just so long as you don't want me to be a volunteer prison visitor.'

'Close. This is a different kind of visit. Nobody else will do. You see I've been to visit Tom Daly's widow. She's in distress, wants to talk to you, says it might help her. You were with him . . . at the end.'

Henry closed his eyes. Hadn't he enough on his plate? But he respected the priest and Tom had been his friend. In all conscience, if the widow wanted to speak to him and it might give her some kind of closure, he'd have to oblige. Apart from the fact it was Father Andrew requesting it, Tom would have expected it of him.

'Well, if you think it will help,' he answered, hoping his lack of enthusiasm didn't show in his voice.

'I think it will.' Henry could hear paper rustling on the other end.' I've got her address here. She's in North Ormesby, in a house now. It's no distance from you.'

142

Henry wrote the address down, promised to visit as soon as he could. After that, the conversation drifted in a desultory fashion, ending with Father Andrew thanking him and promising to call him again soon.

John had come downstairs during their conversation. Henry found him in the kitchen making tea and toast for both of them.

'You feeling better today?' Henry asked as they sat down.

John put down his mug, perched his elbows on the table, cupped his chin in his hands and gave him a sideways glance.

'Feel a big fool. Wish I could turn back the clock, wipe yesterday out.'

Henry chewed thoughtfully on a piece of toast. 'There's not a man alive who hasn't felt like that. A priest once told me to learn from my mistakes and then move on, not look back. Learn to forgive yourself, he said – it wasn't bad advice either.'

'Easy to say,' John said, squinting at him. He sighed, 'Do we have to tell Micky?'

Henry drained his mug, placed a hand on the youth's shoulder.

'Don't worry, Micky's got the years in. He understands more than you think. He barks worse than he bites.'

An hour after their breakfast Henry and John were approaching the community hall. Before they entered Henry glanced across at his companion. The lad's trepidation was written all over his face. Henry wasn't over the moon himself but he knew they were doing the right thing coming here.

'It'll work out,' he said, opening the door, but John still looked burdened with the weight of the world.

A few early birds were already at work on the exercise machines. They walked straight past them to the kitchen. Micky was sitting there staring into space, like a holy man in contemplation. He seemed to snap back into himself when he saw his visitors. Henry thought he detected disappointment in his eyes, guessed he'd already had the bad news, had been chewing it over before they arrived. He decided to broach matters straight off.

'We've come here with a confession, Micky. You won't like what we have to tell you.'

Micky nodded. 'Best you sit, then. This will be a double whammy because I've got bad news as well.' He grinned ruefully. 'We've got the miserable faces; if we had a body we could have a wake.'

Henry rolled his eyes. 'Don't tempt fate, Mick.' He turned to John. 'Go on, tell it the way you told me. Mick'll understand.'

John hunched forward, stared at the surface of the table, began to talk. He never lifted his eyes until he'd finished, then only briefly before he lowered his head like a condemned man putting his head on the block, expecting the executioner's axe to fall.

Micky's eyes flitted to Henry. There was a moment of silent understanding between the two men.

'It took courage to tell the truth, son,' Micky said. 'I'm glad you did because I've already had a phone call from Peter. Those men you saw did break into the house, but fortunately couldn't access the safe, only got away with a couple of paintings not worth a great deal.'

Henry gathered himself. It was his turn now to pour more oil onto the fire.

'I'm sure my rat of a brother was behind it. John told me one of the men looked a bit like me. Using Tonks, who has a grudge, fits his style.' He wanted to add that his brother was a drug dealer, but was so ashamed of his own flesh and blood he couldn't say it to his friend and mentor, especially not in John's presence.

Micky cleared his throat. 'Peter doesn't want you out there again. His wife doesn't like your gypsy background, thinks you might have passed information to dubious friends. Peter himself wasn't of that mind but has given in to her. He wants you to know he's sorry for the way it's turned out.'

Henry couldn't say he was surprised. In truth, he felt sorry for the farmer who'd had such good intentions only to see them go up in smoke, literally and metaphorically. He hoped Mick wasn't paying for the trust he'd invested in him, that his relationship with Fairbrother, who was a sponsor for the community centre, hadn't been damaged.

'I'm so sorry,' he said. 'So sorry for all this.'

'So am I,' John chimed in, his voice no more than a hoarse whisper.

Micky screwed his face up. 'Nah! You're both victims here. Neither to blame.' He pointed to John. 'You redeemed yourself rescuing those horses. Even the Fairbrothers are wondering who the good Samaritan was who let them out. The only trouble is—'

Micky's voice caught in his throat. His face seemed drained of colour. They sensed more bad news coming, mentally braced themselves.

Micky swallowed hard, said it in a rush. 'The chestnut had too much smoke in his lungs. He died later that day.'

Henry's innards felt as though a shark was on the prowl down there taking bites. Tears flooded John's eyes, rolled down his cheeks. He didn't attempt to wipe them away. Both of them had loved that old horse to bits. He'd deserved a better death.

'Something has to happen about this,' Henry said with slow deliberation, remembering how trusting the old chestnut had been.

Micky's hands bunched into fists, as though he wanted to hit out at something, vent his frustration in a way he might once have done in his long gone youth. Finally, he shook his head, unwrapped his fists, laid his hands on the table, fingers extended.

'What can we do, Henry? If we tell the police, Tonks will blame the lad here. Everyone will be told he's a grass. His life will be finished. One way or another, he'd be punished.'

'They shouldn't have done it,' John mumbled, his lips pouting. 'They should pay. I could go to the police if that's the only way – take my chances.'

Henry and Micky exchanged glances. Henry knew how the lad was feeling. What made it even worse for him was his brother's involvement. He felt sullied by their association, however tenuous that was.

'You can't. But maybe I should tell them about my brother.'

The old trainer's stare was withering. 'You need to stay away from the police and you know it. I should never have mentioned them. Grassing isn't the style around here and it certainly isn't the gypsy way, is it?'

Henry sighed audibly. 'It might be that I'll have to deal with Frank myself because, for sure, he's not going to let matters rest.'

'Couldn't you move away for a while?' Mick suggested.

Henry shook his head. 'Probation would have to agree and it would take time.'

A silence settled on the kitchen. There seemed to be no clear solution. Deep down, Henry had a feeling the end was already written, that, no matter how he wanted to avoid it, events were moving inexorably to a confrontation with his brother. Frank couldn't afford to back off. That happening was as likely as South Bank turning into Monte Carlo overnight.

Breaking the depressing silence, he said, 'Frank won't stop until I agree to fight Chip Jackson.'

Micky flared up. 'An illegal fight would be crazy in your position. That's apart from the fact you're not battle hardened – and that takes time. Being fit isn't the same, as you well know.'

'Don't worry, I've no intention,' Henry told him.

Even as he said it, he wondered if he believed it. He was being forced into a corner because people involved with him were being made to suffer. However unpalatable, accepting the fight might be the only way to put a stop to it. Even if he grassed him up, Frank was too wily a character, would have his tracks well covered, and exposing Tonks would almost certainly set the mob against John.

They talked on, but were going around in circles, getting

nowhere fast. Henry suddenly remembered the promise to Father Andrew that he'd go and see Tom Daly's widow. He wanted that visit over and done with as soon as possible. He stood up and John, who'd hardly spoken since hearing about the chestnut's fate, did likewise.

'Something I have to do,' he told the old trainer. Seeing the look on Micky's face, he added, 'Don't worry, it's unrelated. I'll have to mull all this business over, make some decisions. Meanwhile it's best I stay away.'

Micky faced him. 'You don't have to stay away on account of what's happened.'

'Yes, I do, Micky. People are getting trouble because of me and I don't want anything else on my conscience. You've helped me and I don't want you suffering.'

Micky opened his mouth, aborted his answer when he saw the stubborn set of Henry's jaw.

Henry stretched out his hand. 'Whatever you hear, believe the best of me.'

As they shook, Mick forced a grin which contradicted the sadness in his eyes.

'Didn't I always, son? Didn't I always?'

North Ormesby, where Bridget Daly resided, was a stone's throw from South Bank, just a smidgeon more up-market. Leaving John to find his own way back to the house, Henry hopped on a bus, the first time he'd used public transport since his release. Sitting amongst people leading normal, everyday lives brought back memories and a comforting sense that the world was going on as it always had. Yet, for him, life was far from back to normality. Mary had been correct. Coming back had been a mistake. But if he hadn't, he wouldn't have seen a softer side to his father he'd never dreamed existed. While those glimpses hadn't reconciled him to the old man, he couldn't feel the same bitter hatred he'd built over those prison years, even felt a pang of sympathy for his deteriorating health. He wondered if, in spite of his denials, his reason for coming back, in some twisted way a psychologist would make much of, had to do with his father and brother living in South Bank.

The house was only a short walk from the bus stop. Henry rang the bell, waited until it opened just enough for a woman's gaunt face to appear. Her apprehensive eyes reminded him of a mouse peeping out of a hole afraid the cat's paw was poised to take a swipe.

'It's Henry Torrance, Bridget,' he announced gently. 'Father Andrew sent me.'

She opened the door slowly, lethargically, as though the action was costing her energy she could ill afford to expend. Now that he saw her in her full glory he was taken aback, had to hide it. Her hair was a tangled mess. She wore a creased skirt, a food-stained cardigan which she was holding around herself like armour against the outside world. He'd met her once, briefly, years ago when she was a young teenager. This was a far cry from his memory of her, and from the pretty, vibrant woman in the picture Tom had taken pride in showing him.

'Come in, Henry,' she said, stepping back and wafting her hand in a beckoning manner. He followed her through to the lounge, wondering what he was getting himself into, how any words he could utter were going to make a difference to this woman. She looked as though she needed more than words.

The curtains were only open a little, leaving the room in a half gloom. It felt like a funeral parlour. Bridget gestured casually at a chair and he sat down. A coffee table, burdened with dirty plates and cups, lay in front of him. The meagre shaft of light squeezing through the curtains alighted on a television set in the corner, showed a thick layer of dust on a screen scored by finger marks.

She lowered herself into the chair opposite. Henry shifted uncomfortably, wondered if he should introduce the subject of Tom's death without preliminaries, or leave it to her. She rescued him by speaking first.

'I know this place is a mess,' she said, her voice lethargic. 'I haven't bothered with it since – since Tom's death. Have to make an effort, won't I?'

He cleared his throat. 'That's understandable. Can't be easy for you.'

They were platitudes he was giving her and he knew it. What else was there? He wasn't a bereavement counsellor. Best to get to the point quickly.

She was staring into the fireplace, didn't look at him as he spoke.

'Tom talked about you a lot, Bridget.'

A ghost of a smile played on her lips. She wiped her eyes with a sleeve, drying away tears. Henry was relieved when she at last looked at him and spoke in a stronger voice.

'He talked about you as well. Said you helped him cope in – that place.'

Henry shrugged diffidently. 'He was a pal. Knew him from way back. We grew closer in prison.'

Once again Bridget retired into her shell. Her whole

body seemed to go limp and listless. Henry didn't know what to say, just waited. Then, suddenly, as though an electric charge had passed through her, she sat bolt upright. She looked like an actress with stage fright in the full glare of the spotlight.

Henry thought she was oblivious to his presence. He waited more than a minute in silence before her eyelids fluttered like delicate butterfly wings and she met his stare.

'You must think I'm a terrible woman,' she said. 'I'm sure you know I bought drugs for Tom and arranged for them to be smuggled inside.'

How should he respond? Should he tell the widow he thought it had been a crazy thing to do, at the very best misguided? Aware of her fragile state, he settled for a toned-down version.

'It wasn't a good idea, not really. But I know how Tom was. He wouldn't help himself. I tried—'

'I used all our money,' she interrupted.

Henry nodded, 'Yes, he told me.'

Bridget's eyes bulged, as though they were going to spring out of their sockets. Her laugh was disconcerting, self-mocking, like a crow's.

'We hadn't much. For a long time I resorted to other means to get him his drugs.'

Henry shifted uncomfortably in his chair. He'd heard the regret, the self recrimination in Bridget's voice, sensed she was about to make a confession, hoped not. Why should he be the recipient? Why not Father Andrew whose business it was to hear such things?

'Other means?' he echoed, in spite of himself.

Bridget dug her fingers into her knees. 'I knew how

151

much Tom needed his fix, wanted to help him.' She drew her fingers up her thighs, digging the nails in as though she deliberately wanted to feel pain, hurt herself. 'I met Jet Jackson on a visit to one of the gypsy camps. I'd known him a long time before I met Tom and I told him my problem. He said he had ways of smuggling the drugs inside – so I paid him.'

'Until the money ran out?'

She nodded, drew back her lips, showed her teeth. It gave her the feral look of a huntress.

Henry had to prompt her again. 'And after the money ran out?'

'Jet had always fancied me. He supplied Tom for a while – until I was in his debt, then said my debt was Tom's and he would have to be punished if he couldn't pay, that he could stop that happening and continue to supply Tom if I went out with him.'

Henry studied the woman, the anguish on her face. How easy it was to be trapped when you were weak, made bargains with men who had not an ounce of compassion. She was looking at him now, a plea for understanding in her eyes.

'I did it for Tom and because . . . I was lonely. It was all right at first, then he grew tired of me, became abusive, finally dropped me like a stone.'

Henry's memory flashed back to the cell, Tom's suffering in those last days, the beating he'd taken in the shower. His wife, in her foolishness, had been helping him down the road to nowhere.

'That's when they stopped supplying Tom,' Henry said. 'And you had to tell him it was because you'd run out of money – which was half the truth.'

Bridget pulled at the tangle of her hair. He sensed there was more to come and he waited silently, giving her time.

'There's something I need to know,' she said hesitantly. 'It's killing me not knowing. You knew Tom better than anyone near the end.' She caught the throb in her throat. 'I'd like the truth – no matter what.'

Henry thought he could guess what was coming. 'If I can help, I will.'

She focused on the corner of the room, clasped her hands together in her lap trying to compose herself.

'I need to know' – she began – 'I need you to tell me whether Tom knew— When he killed himself did he—'

As her question died on her lips, Henry reached across, grasped her hand. She dragged her gaze back to him. Tears were dropping from her eyes. One hot tear landed on his outstretched hand.

'No, Bridget, Tom never knew about you and Jet. Right till the end he talked about you in loving terms.'

Her shoulders started to shake. More tears fell. Henry squeezed her hand harder.

'Why then?' she mumbled, making an effort to control herself.

'You know why,' he told her, his voice adamant. 'The dragon swallowed him. Tom was hooked, couldn't give it up. Even without you, he'd have found a way. I tried but he was too far down the road.' He shook his head in exasperation as he remembered. 'I don't know. Maybe he started too young.'

It wasn't strictly the truth. There'd been a chance, a slim one but nevertheless a chance that, if he'd volunteered for the drug free wing Tom could have been weaned off them. It would have been hard but, in the end, perhaps more loving not to comply with his demands. But he wasn't going to tell his widow that now. She was paying a price, suffering for her mistakes. He wasn't going to add to her woes.

His words seemed to be a comfort to her because she stopped crying and dabbed at her tears. Henry slid his hand away from hers, sat back. When he thought she'd regained a little composure he spoke again.

'Tom wouldn't like to see you like this, you know. He liked light and laughter, wouldn't like to see someone he loved living in a mausoleum. Forgive me, but he'd tell you to open those curtains and let the light in, to try to get on with life.'

He was sure he'd gone too far, but it had come from the heart and was truly what her husband would have told her. She seemed to take it well, didn't launch into a tirade telling him to mind his own business and what did he know about her grief. As if emerging from a cocoon, aware of her surroundings for the first time, she swivelled her head to all four corners of the room in turn.

'I haven't been able to concentrate,' she said. He noticed a slight slackening of tension in her facial muscles. 'You've no idea what it means to me to know Tom had no knowledge that I'd let him down, that it wasn't the reason—' She left the rest unsaid.

Henry felt it was time to leave. He'd done all he could here. Bridget seemed, if far from sparkling, more alive. As he started to rise, she held up her hand to stop him. He sank back into the chair again wondering what else there was to talk about, only too aware he had pressure in his own life to sort out that would take more than talking.

'You were Tom's friend and you've helped me by coming here,' she said. 'Maybe it won't mean anything to you, but I think there's something you should know.'

Henry exercised his patience. He didn't think there could be anything she could tell him that would interest him right now.

'Once when I was out with Jet,' she continued, wrinkling her nose with distaste at the memory, 'he drove us to a farm near Saltburn. There was a guard on the gate, I remember. Jet drove us down a long track, parked well away from the house, told me not to get out. That was when I saw your brother with Daniel and Terry Jackson.'

Henry wasn't too surprised to hear it, given what his father had told him. He gave a snort. 'Must have been a pig farm.'

Bridget continued, 'Daniel Jackson picked up a spade and dug into a pile of manure lying in the yard. I watched him pull a package out of the dung and hand it to Frank.'

Henry blew out his cheeks. He didn't have to engage his brain much to figure out what was in the package. Bridget's story was merely confirming his brother's drug link with the Jacksons.

'They let you see them doing that?'

Bridget shook her head. 'The car was a good distance away and I sank low in the seat. Jet soon came back and we were gone.'

'So one little piggy got careless and let you see the other piggies going to the market for their drugs,' Henry mused. 'Good job they didn't see you.'

Bridget sighed. 'Anyway, I thought you'd like to know about your brother. Maybe you can get him away from them before he's in too deep.'

Henry didn't tell her Frank was already in too deep, had touched bottom, his feet stuck in the mud, murky waters swirling all around him.

'Thanks,' he said. 'I'll try. Did you happen to get the name of that farm?'

Bridget thought a moment. 'Brass Farm. Yes – that was definitely it. But you could hardly see the sign from the road. Probably they didn't want anyone to.'

Henry smiled at the double irony. Where there was muck there was brass and the Jacksons had plenty of brass neck to brazen anything out.

This time, when he stood up, she rose with him. 'Appreciate you telling me about Frank,' he said, making for the door.

She followed him onto the doorstep. When he turned towards her she seemed more enlivened, like an animal awakening from long hibernation, the light of life reviving in the eyes. She pinned him now with those same eyes.

'I loved Tom, you know. Even when I was stupid enough to go out with Jet the main part of me thought I was doing it for him.'

He leaned forward, instinctively kissed her cheek. 'Consider that from Tom and try to move on. It's what he would have wanted.'

As he walked to the bus stop, it struck him how conscience was a terrible thing, didn't always show at the first transgression, lurked until changed circumstances forced you to confront it head on. Of course, there always

had to be the exceptions who proved the rule. Frank and
the Jacksons? Did any of them have a conscience? If so
disuse must have shrunk it to the size of a pea. Or was
even that a gross exaggeration?

Riding back on the bus, he mulled over everything
Bridget had told him. The Jacksons were engaged in an evil
trade and Frank was no better than them. Their nefarious
activities were leaving a trail of destruction, damaged
lives. Could he sit back or was it time to go on the attack?
The more he thought about it Brass Farm could well be the
key to bringing the empire down on its own head and
Bridget had handed it to him on a plate.

That night, sleep evaded Henry. He'd been out with Mary
earlier but was distracted all evening. She'd caught on and,
against his better judgement, he'd told her what he'd
decided and, in spite of her heartfelt protestations didn't
let her dissuade him. When he left her, he promised he'd
keep her informed, then rang Micky and arranged to
borrow his car next day.

Rising early, he told John he had business to attend to,
something he could only do alone, would be away all day
so not to worry about him. He loaded his haversack into
the boot, placed binoculars and a camera he'd borrowed
from Mary on the passenger seat.

He drove to Saltburn, purchased an ordinance survey
map of the area, then parked on the sea cliffs and found
Brass Farm on the map. He saw that the land surrounding
the farm buildings was mainly flat, not a good thing for his
purposes, but there was a line of green trees that ran onto
the land. The line ended 200 metres from the buildings and

from there, according to the contour lines, a small gully slanted towards the farm.

When he'd finished with the map, he looked out to sea. It was a monotonous grey colour today, white mouthed breakers rising like predators out of the grey to bite down like teeth He didn't envy the trawlermen out on a day like this. But, then again, would they envy him? He was hoping for a catch of his own; sharks who'd emerged from that same sea aeons ago to walk on the land in the guise of humans.

It was a two-mile drive to Brass Farm. Just as Bridget had informed him the sign was half hidden. He didn't see the guard as he drove past. Not wanting to draw attention to himself, he didn't turn his head to look for him either. But once he was past he glanced in the mirror, caught a slight movement in trees growing well back from the road. Someone was in there keeping an eye out.

He used the back roads, found the finger of trees shown on the map, parked the car. Rucksack over his shoulder, he started out, to all appearances an enthusiastic, lone rambler.

Ten minutes later he was at the extremity of the finger of trees, flat land all around. But his map reading had not let him down; just as he'd expected there was a depression in the ground twenty metres ahead. Using it, he could work his way to within 125 metres of the buildings without being seen.

Dragging the rucksack behind him, he bellied his way towards the shallow gully, slid down into it, moved along in a low crouch towards the buildings. When the gully became almost too shallow to hide him, he halted, removed his sleeping bag from the rucksack, laid the camera, binoculars and a flask of coffee laced with whisky beside him. Next he arranged a screen of grass and mud at face level to help camouflage him when he used the binoculars, then settled down to watch the farm.

An hour dragged by and he began to wonder whether it was going to prove a fruitless exercise. Then a car came down the main track. Through the binoculars, he recognized the figure who climbed out. It was a drug dealer he'd seen during his time in prison. Henry's hopes revived, especially when Danny Jackson stepped out of the main building to meet him and their arms went around each other's shoulders as though they were bosom pals. Watching the display made him want to puke. These were vicious men putting on a show of *hail fellow well met* because it suited their purpose, but it was all affectation, all front, and they knew it. They would be prepared to cut the other's throat at the drop of a hat if a big enough profit was involved.

They entered the house for a few minutes. When they emerged, Danny went straight to a pile of manure piled up against the side of a shed, picked up a shovel. Henry permitted himself a smile of satisfaction, silently thanked Bridget Daly as he used his camera to capture the gypsy digging into the dung and pulling out a bag which he handed to the dealer. He was still snapping away as they walked to the car and did that hugging thing all over again. Finally, the ritual over, the dealer got back in his car and drove off.

Henry relaxed, rewarded himself with a hot drink. So far, so good, he thought as the liquid warmed him; Bridget had been right on the ball and there was still time for more developments. Though it was going to be a long day, he figured it could turn out to be a profitable one for him.

Another visitor, this time one he didn't recognize, arrived exactly an hour later. The artificial emotional stuff was on display again and Henry captured it on the camera, with Danny excavating the manure again and handing over his little gift. After that, it was back to waiting until, mid afternoon, Terry and Jet Jackson came out into the yard and entered an outbuilding to emerge moments later carrying a sack which they buried in the manure. Henry kept clicking away. This was an unexpected little bonus and he prayed all the photographs he was taking would come out clearly.

Evening drew in. Down at the farmhouse, someone put the lights on and pulled the curtains. Henry, stiff and cold, crawled into the sleeping bag and drained the remnants from the flask. He still had work to do, but he needed the cover of darkness to carry it out. He managed to doze off, awoke to find the lights from the farm were beacons in a sea of darkness. It was time for his next move.

He packed his rucksack, left it in the gully to collect later, then, glad to be on the move, started across the field towards the buildings. This was the dangerous part of his plan, but it would provide him with the icing on the cake if he could pull it off.

For a long time Henry stood watching the yard, motionless like a creature of the night, senses alert to every nuance of shape and sound, praying there was no guard or, equally daunting, a watchdog. When he was satisfied, he covered the last few yards, heading into the yard, knowing if they caught him he'd be lucky to see another dawn.

He guessed his nose could have guided him because, close up, before he saw the manure, the stench hit him. They'd chosen well; nobody would go near that dung heap voluntarily. He searched for the spade Danny used, couldn't find it, so got down, tunnelled with his hands, the smell making him nauseous. He dragged a large bag clear, opened it, extracted smaller bags of white powder, snapped away with his camera. All the while he cast wary glances at the house. No sign of movement there, thank God! Sweating, in spite of the cold, he put everything back the way he'd found it. Finally, satisfied nobody would know he'd been there, he started back the way he'd come.

He was halfway across the yard when the door opened and shaft of light sliced the night wide open. Henry froze. Like a moth compelled by sudden brightness, he could only stare for a moment. Snapping out of it, he took two steps backwards into the dark, conscious of his boot scraping on the cobbled yard, the thud of his heart.

A man's silhouette appeared in the doorway. His shadow seemed huge, a night monster blocking the light spilling from the door. The shadow grew longer, was swallowed by the darkness as the figure stepped out of the arc of light. Henry fought his panic, forced himself to stand still. Where was the man now? He had no idea!

Suddenly, twenty yards to his left, a match flared, followed by the red glow of a cigarette dancing in the dark like a firefly. It came from the direction he needed to go, meant the man was blocking his route out of the yard. He edged backwards, smelled the dung heap, realized he was back where he'd started, could retreat no further because of the wall behind the heap. Like a midget heat-seeking missile, the red firefly began heading in his direction. Henry figured he only had a few seconds before the man would be on top of him. Desperate, he did the only thing that came to mind. Stuffing the camera inside his jacket, he launched himself into the dung and burrowed in like a mole.

The smell was foul, worse than any sewer, the urge to gag overwhelming. He daren't move his head, used his ears to try to pin point the man's position. After what seemed an eternity of silence, he heard a boot scraping on a cobblestone. It was so close its owner must be almost on top of him. He sucked in his cheeks, battling against the nausea. Not to be outdone, his body cranked up the tension so that he was conscious of every muscle tightening. He forced himself to listen but the only sound was an owl hooting out there in the night, as though it could see his artifice and was amused by the human drama played out in its own preserve.

Close by, came a guttural sound. Somebody clearing his throat. By now the urge to leap out of the pile and take his chances was almost irresistible but he forced himself to wait. Then he heard a whistled tune, an old gypsy song he recognized, one he'd heard his mother sing. He knew the man was on the move because the melody grew gradually fainter.

A minute later the door slammed and he took a chance. Like a creature slithering from a primordial mud heap, he dragged himself from the dung, stood and gulped down fresh air. He quickly rearranged the manure, then cautiously started back the way he'd come. Lady Luck had almost deserted him at the last moment, but fortunately returned to him again in the nick of time and he walked clear.

Before he drove back, he covered his seat with newspapers that he found in the boot of the car and opened all the windows. The smell was still sickening but he consoled himself that, unlike the rotten stink of those corrupt souls he'd witnessed pursuing their vile trade today, he could wash it off when he got home.

John Walsh froze. The spoonful of cornflakes made it only halfway to his mouth. Henry smiled at his reaction and drank his tea. He was feeling better, enjoying his breakfast now that he'd had a good night's rest and was cleansed of that smell of manure which he'd had to endure on the drive back last night.

John found his voice. 'You're serious? You want to take me with you when you go?'

Henry nodded. 'Have a good think about it. You don't need to answer right now. Besides, the best laid plans of mice and men. Everything could fall in on my head. There's a lot of people have to agree.'

'It's a big risk, what you're doing,' John said. 'But it's a way out.' He put the spoon back in the bowl, stared out of the window, added ruefully. 'And a way out for me too if you can pull it off.'

Henry sat back. 'Don't mistake me. I don't relish what I'm going to do. Sometimes there's only one choice, however unpalatable, however much it goes against the grain.'

163

John's gaze came back from the window. 'I don't need to think,' he said. 'I'll go.'

'That's settled then.' Henry rose from the table. 'Now I need to get a shift on. I've a busy day. I rang my dear brother soon as I got out of bed. I'm meeting him outside the church in half an hour.'

He left John at the breakfast table, put his jacket on and stepped out into a cold morning. Micky's car was parked outside but he decided to walk. Later he'd vacuum the interior, return it in the same condition he'd received it.

Frank was sitting on the church wall waiting for him. Behind the wall, gravestones stood in sombre lines, an army of the dead keeping silent watch. Henry wasn't as superstitious as a lot of gypsies, but a shiver ran down his spine. Part of him would have liked to have made one last appeal to Frank, but the rot had gone too far. His brother would just see it as a weakness.

As Henry approached him, Frank smiled, as though he was confident Henry had come here to capitulate, accede to his demands at last. Studying his face close up, though, that smile belied a dullness in his eyes.

'Seen the light at last, have you?' Frank's tone was arrogant, but a nerve pulsing above his eyebrow gave him away. Beneath the bravado, there was anxiety.

'You've got your way, Frank,' Henry said, affecting a weary, defeated tone. 'I'm tired. I just want you off my back – out of my life – forever.'

'Took you long enough to come round,' Frank grunted, rubbing his hands together. 'Here's how it goes, kidda. If you win, you get twenty thousand – I get the same amount. Our nearest and dearest gets his forty grand back. You lose, we all lose – everything.'

Henry cocked an eyebrow. 'Doesn't sound your kind of deal. You know I've been out a long time – the odds on me winning can't be that good, can they?'

Frank shrugged. 'This wasn't down to me. The old man was foolish enough to lead us into this one.'

Henry shrugged. 'Suppose so.'

He knew what he knew. Frank was aware he would win either way because as long as he fought Chip he would avoid punishment, or death perhaps, at the hands of the Jacksons.

A momentary spark lit Frank's eyes. 'If you threw the fight, maybe I could fix something so we get a share of the betting.'

Henry thought about it. It would be one way of ensuring he didn't take a real battering. But it didn't feel right.

'Five years hasn't taken away all my dignity,' he snapped back. 'Not that you would know anything about dignity.'

Frank snorted. 'You know me so well, Brother. Let's hope you're good enough, or the old man's savings go down the shoot.'

Henry couldn't help himself. 'Nice that you're so concerned about the old man.'

Frank's eyes flashed in temper but he didn't answer.

Henry said 'Is he going to be there, the old man?'

Frank shook his head. 'He's as weak as a kitten, taking the big count but just won't stay down, the silly old goat.'

That came as a shock. For sure, all the signs had been there when his father came to the house, but he'd been so set against him he hadn't allowed himself to see how near the end he was. Now he realized his father had made a big effort. But there was no time to dwell on that. Frank was watching him and the matter at hand needed all his concentration.

'I take it the arrangements have been made.'

Frank put his thumb up. 'Friday night's the night. I'll pick you up about seven with the money. You make sure you're ready.'

'And the venue?'

Frank narrowed his eyes suspiciously. 'You don't need to know. The Jacksons will tell me and all the punters at the last minute. That way there's less chance of the law hearing about it.'

Henry wasn't surprised. It was standard practice to keep the whereabouts of a big fight quiet.

'The punters won't even know where they are when they get there.' Frank added. 'They'll be picked up in minibuses with the windows blacked out and it'll be isolated.'

'That's us then,' Henry said. 'All done and dusted. You've managed to get your way, Frank. But there'll be a day of reckoning. There always is for people like you.'

Frank laughed, but in those dull eyes there was no real mirth.

'Sounds like you got religion, kid. Heard you had. Hope it doesn't affect your performance. Me, I'm just glad you came around to my way of thinking after a little – earthly persuasion.' He jabbed a finger in Henry's direction. 'Friday!'

Henry watched him walk away. Just for a moment he saw his mother's gait, the same slight roll of the shoulders and it made him feel worse about what he had to do now.

After his meeting with Frank, the next few days dragged by for Henry, though he was busy enough setting everything up. Mary proved just how much she believed in him by agreeing he should take his plan all the way to make them safe, even though she was worried stiff about him and it would turn her life upside down. Without her assent he couldn't have done it because it would have meant losing her.

Friday evening arrived and dead on the dot Frank drew up outside the house driving a van. There could be no going back now and Henry knew it. For better or worse, the dice were cast.

'Mary will be coming for you,' he told John as he stepped out the door. The youth looked at him as though the end of the world was nigh.

Frank jerked his head, indicating he should ride in the back. He threw his bag inside, climbed in after it. His brother pointed to the passenger seat. Henry stretched his neck, saw a leather bag lying there.

'I've brought the old man's money. It's down to you now whether we keep it.'

Henry splayed his legs on the floor, not wanting to stiffen up. He'd put in a couple of extra training sessions, geared specifically to bare knuckle fighting, but was aware that he was only seventy five per cent ready physically for a fight like this. There was the mental side to consider too; the last time he'd fought, a man had died. How would that affect him? Hopefully, he would never get even near to the point where he had to do serious damage.

Frank broke an extended silence, his voice sarcastic. 'The old feller wanted to watch his golden boy perform but I refused to bring him. Boy did he kick off! Weak as he is, he's still got a mouth on him. That's how he got us into this, with his mouth and his faith in his golden boy.'

'And you couldn't stop him?'

'You've seen him in drink. Once he shook hands there was no going back. Too much faith in you, like always.'

Frank's face was caught in a car's headlights. Henry figured there should have been some obvious signpost in the features to indicate it was the face of a habitual liar. His father had learned the truth but far too late.

'Gypsy honour was involved, eh! You'd know all about that, Frank.'

His brother half-turned his head, ignored the barb. 'Got to move with the times, kidda. The old ways are dying.'

'Some things are worth preserving,' Henry said.

The van swung off the main road, began to bounce and rock from side to side, jolting Henry's muscles. He figured they must be close to their destination. His stomach muscles tensed involuntarily with the knowledge that soon he'd have to perform.

Suddenly, like a ghost manifesting itself out of darkness, a man appeared in the main beam, his hands in the air. Frank braked hard, wound down the window as he approached.

A pudgy face, topped by carrot hair, peered inside. 'It's yourself, Frank,' an Irish accent declared. 'Got the lad with you?'

Frank leaned to the side, jerked a thumb over his

shoulder. A torch beam lit Henry's face, dazzling him. It inspected the interior of the vehicle, then withdrew.

'Another hundred yards, left at the trees, and you're there,' the voice informed.

Frank muttered something unintelligible and the van rattled off. The trees appeared in the headlights, the track curved sharply. A little further and three men holding lanterns appeared, beyond them an outline of buildings, one much larger than the rest. They drove into a yard where minibuses and cars were parked. The men with lanterns guided Frank into a space behind a row of minibuses.

'Good turn out by the looks of it,' Frank commented.

When they got out the three men came to them. Henry could see they were all burly fellows obviously brought in to handle security.

'You're to follow us,'one of them said.

Henry forced a smile. 'I always follow where beauty leads.'

Their sullen looks told him they didn't like his cheek. They made for the largest building, but before they got there a car door opened blocking their path. Daniel Jackson and his two sons got out of a Mercedes. All three were dressed identically in long coats, scarves coiled around their necks. The lantern light distorted their features, gave them a feral look, like vampires in a horror film Henry thought, voracious for blood – his blood.

'Long time no see,' Danny hissed.

'Those coats were out of fashion before I went inside,' Henry said. 'Didn't know they were making a comeback. Thought that was only me.'

Danny smirked. 'Smart mouth, eh! Just like your old

169

man. And look where it got him.'

Jet couldn't hold back. 'Chip will soon shut it for him.'

'In this game,' Henry said, eyeing him, 'talk is cheap, especially when it comes from those who haven't the guts to fight, the watchers of the world.'

Terry muttered, 'Taken you long enough to work yourself up to it.'

Henry ignored him, held up his bag. 'Need a place to get changed and to speak to you three alone.' He pointed a finger at Frank, continued, 'Alone means without him there.'

Danny frowned. 'What could we have to discuss?'

'It's a business matter, big money involved. And I mean *big* money.'

Frank's eyes were all over him, resentful. Henry knew he was keeping quiet only because the Jacksons had a hold over him.

'Thought you had enough business to occupy you for one night,' Danny said.

'Life goes on after tonight.'

Jet laughed. 'And after tonight you might not be able to talk proper. That's it, isn't it?'

Danny was quiet, weighing him up. Under his outward cool, Henry's stomach was churning. Finally Danny made his decision, pointed to a smaller building.

'We'll talk in the barn. After we're done you can change there. But let's make it snappy. We don't want the punters getting anxious.'

They headed for the barn. After a few yards Terry turned on his heel, called back to Frank.

'You hold on to that money, big brother. We're going to

170

let you hold all of it tonight. Show how much we trust you.' He cackled like an old crone. 'Downside is, it'll be all the harder when you have to hand it over.'

When Danny switched the lights on, Henry saw that the barn was a throw back, hay strewn haphazardly about the floor, rusting, antiquated farm implements lying everywhere. He walked ahead, dumped his bag on a bale of hay, unzipped it. Using his body to mask the movement, he removed the mobile phone from the bag, slid it under the straw. Slipping his jacket off, he laid that down on top.

'We didn't come to watch a striptease,' Jet called out.

Henry turned, walked back to them, concentrated his gaze on the father, ignoring his sons.

'So what's this about?' Danny asked. 'Big money, you said.'

Henry inhaled deeply. So much depended on how well he sold it.

'A drug deal is what it's about – a big one.' Henry knew the words were coming out of his mouth, but they sounded surreal, his voice seeming to belong to someone else. 'It's too big for me. I've asked around and people say you can handle it.'

Danny raised a wary eyebrow. 'Spit it out and we'll see.'

'In prison I made a contact,' Henry began, drawing in a breath,'a big shot who has family in London. The family are looking to extend their business beyond the capital. They can provide regular loads of pure heroin worth a hundred grand or more.'

Danny looked impressed. 'That's heavy. How regular is regular?'

'Monthly, according to my guy. Their idea is to make the exchange somewhere halfway between here and London – at night – in a service station.'

Henry could tell he'd piqued their interest. But they'd be fools not to be suspicious and they weren't fools when it came to money. Far from it.

Jet came back at him. 'What's in it for you?'

'Five grand every time there's an exchange. The guy was close to me in prison, wants me to be the go-between.'

Danny puffed out his cheeks, let the air out audibly. Henry hoped his greed would get the better of him.

'A hundred grand of pure heroin is worth a lot more on the streets. I got to be interested.'

'How do we know this isn't a set up?' Terry chirped.

Jet said,' Yeah! They could take our money and run.'

'Happened to us recently,' Terry added. 'Feller we gave a bit of rein fouled up. He's suffering for it right now.' He smirked knowingly. 'You might even know him.'

'My guy says his boss will meet with you beforehand, anywhere you want. That way you'll know he's up front.' Henry waited, watched their faces, knew their greed was vying with their dislike of him. 'So, what do you think?'

Danny made a decision 'No harm if we meet the guy. If we're satisfied, we'll do it.'

Henry said gruffly, 'Fair enough.'

Terry pulled a face. 'You got strange timing, Torrance. Doing this just before you're about to take a hammering?'

'Call it an insurance policy. It's in your interest to make sure your man leaves me with all my faculties. I'll need them to negotiate the deal.'

Jet smiled. 'So not so confident after all.'

'Just covering all the angles. He might throw a lucky one.'

Danny looked at his watch. 'We're done here. Let's get on with it. We don't want to keep the punters waiting.'

'Right then,' Henry said. 'Let me finish changing and I'll be there.'

As they strode though the darkness, long coats flowing behind them, Jet Jackson voiced his reservations.

'We're doing business with a man who killed Bull. Ain't that . . . disrespectful?'

His father grabbed his arm. 'Bull's death was a freak happening, one of those things. People built Torrance up afterwards. That's what irks – that's the insult.' He eased his grip. 'Business is business, son. Sentiment is sentiment. Don't confuse the two. Don't never sniff at nothing if there's money in it.'

Terry said, 'He's right, Brother. That's how we've made a pile, ain't it?'

They continued past the lantern holders to the main building. Before they stepped inside, Danny put his arms around his sons' shoulders, drew them close.

'If it works out, know who I'm going to insist goes all alone on that first exchange?'

Both sons shook their heads.

'Frank Torrance, that's who.'

'You'd trust him with that?' Jet said, disbelieving. 'After he tried it on?'

Terry got the idea, mirrored his father's smirk as he explained it to his brother.

'We'll be there though, won't we, at a distance, mob

handed, watching our money? Anything goes wrong, Frank's first in the firing line. Right, Pa?'

'Right, son!'

Jet's smiled. 'I like that.'

'Business is business,' Danny said. 'You can't be soft. Frankie boy thinks after tonight he's off the hook, but he ain't.'

Terry looked back at the barn. 'You don't suppose our new business partner has a chance against Chip, do you?'

Danny shook his head. 'Been out of it too long and he knows it. Tell Chip to work him over good, but leave him with his . . . faculties.'

'Let's get in there,' Jet said. 'I can't wait.'

Henry put on an old pair of jeans, took his shirt off, slipped his jacket over his bare torso as protection against the night air. The phone under the straw was the latest in surveillance technology, had a built-in recording device, which had captured the conversation with the Jacksons, and a signalling device he'd activated as soon as they'd left the barn.

The lantern holders saw him emerge, watched in silence as he headed for the main building. Above him, the moon was a perfect curve like a scimitar hanging over the earth. A feeling of loneliness swept over Henry. In the past, his father would have been behind him when he made his entrance, Frank next to his father, so silent you wouldn't have a clue what was going through his head. It had been a family affair and in his youthful naivety he'd thought that meant something. This time he was alone as he approached the door. Behind him, one of the men found the courage to call out.

'He's gonna kill you, Torrance.'

Henry ignored it. Once he was inside they'd be shouting worse things. He stepped through the door. After the darkness, the glare was like awakening into bright sunshine.

His eyes took a moment to adjust. When they did, he realized the building was larger than he'd thought. Immediately ahead, stretching for a good thirty metres, was empty concrete floor. Beyond that, the crowd waited, making a low humming sound. Over the heads, as though it was the centre piece of worshipful attention, he could see a cage shaped like a bell. His anger stirred at the sight; cages were for wild animals. Nobody had mentioned he'd be fighting in one and he didn't like the idea, that feeling of being trapped. It was too much like being in prison.

As he started forward, the door slammed behind him, the noise echoing like a gunshot. The hum of the crowd died away. As one, the heads turned in his direction. He kept moving, hating those inquisitive gazes, the cool appraisal of his body as though he was an exotic beast bred for their pleasure, not a man.

He could feel the excitement in the air like a charge of electricity. The hum started again, rose to new levels. Necks craned to get a better view. He was tempted to lower his head, avoid all those stares, but he held his chin high as they parted to let him through.

He was conscious many of the men were well dressed, reeked of money, that the few women present could have been clones. They were long-legged and lissom, expensively dressed, dripping with jewellery and hanging on the arms

175

of their partners a bit too enthusiastically, as though they felt that they were accessories, as easily disposed of as the losing fighter if they weren't careful to please. Here and there, a voice called his name, but it meant nothing more to Henry than wasted sweat.

At last he was through the crowd and the cage dominated his vision. He thought he could see bloodstains on the bars. Frank was with the Jacksons and beside them, bare chested, Chip Jackson stood like a young colossus. As Henry advanced their eyes locked and he saw his opponent was taller, probably a stone or more heavier. In the past, he'd fought heavier men but they'd invariably carried body fat, which ultimately taxed their stamina, slowed them down. Chip showed no signs of any excess weight; he was honed. Henry knew instantly he was a man totally dedicated to his fighting profession.

As he came closer, he saw that Chip was younger than he looked from a distance. His hair was dyed blond, but all the Jacksons' genetic features showed in his face. Just for a second, he thought he could see Bull Jackson staring out at him from Chip's eyes and a cold tingling sensation crept down his spine as the memory of the night that had changed his life resurrected itself.

Frank was holding the bag containing their father's money. Now Danny handed him another bag to hold.

'You're the banker, Frank. That's our bundle. I'll be right next to you, sunshine, ready to take it back soon as your brother there is done for, so don't get carried away.'

'Rules!' Henry snapped.

Danny faced him. 'No gouging, no hitting a man when he's down. Fight's finished when one of you can't stand.

176

Winner takes all.' He pointed to a fat man in a waistcoat who had joined them. 'Jack's the referee. He's known to one and all as a fair man.'

'OK,' Henry said, hoping nothing he'd just heard would be relevant anyway.

'All bets are laid,' Jet said, rubbing his hands together. 'Let's get it on!'

Henry started towards the cage but Frank restrained him, leaned in close, spoke in a low voice.

'If you win, we get out of here quick with the money. Things can turn nasty. I've seen it happen.'

Henry took no notice, dismissed him with a look. He had other things on his mind. Besides, it wasn't going to work out the way Frank was imagining, not the way any of these morons was imagining.

The cage door swung open. Chip came up beside him, thrust his face so close to Henry's he could smell garlic on his breath.

'Tonight is for Bull,' he rasped, spittle shooting from his mouth.

Henry squared his shoulders, refusing to be intimidated. 'Bull's death was a pure accident, a bad piece of luck, nothing more. I can't help what people say about it.' He pointed at the cage. 'Nothing that happens when we step in there will bring Bull back either and that's a pity.'

The regretful words and calm tone confused Chip, but it soon passed.

'The man told me not to destroy you, but that still leaves me plenty of room to enjoy myself.' He stepped to one side. 'After you, Torrance.'

They stood in the middle of the cage, facing each other.

Like a classroom of kids who excitedly anticipate the playtime bell when all their pent-up energy can be released, the crowd turned up the volume. Most were shouting for Chip. Henry knew he'd been out too long for them to risk big money on him. Truth be told, he'd probably bet against himself.

The referee stepped between them, stuck out his chest, repeated the rules, added a spiel of his own. Henry half listened, hoping he wasn't making the biggest mistake of his life. If that device in the mobile did the job it was supposed to, everything would be all right and he'd only have to survive a minute or two. But he was well aware he was depending on others doing their bit.

The referee signalled the start. Henry retreated, putting his mind in a zone where nothing existed except his opponent. Chip started circling. Henry thought he'd decided to wait for him to make the first move and that suited him fine. The longer he could string this out without coming to blows the better.

The crowd was of a different mind. As both fighters danced and feinted, they called out for action. Chip reacted to their baiting, took a few preliminary swings, which Henry evaded easily. A germ of doubt came into Chip's eyes, burgeoned into an angry gleam. Henry could see he was letting the crowd's impatience affect him. How long would he wait before launching an all or nothing assault?

'Pair of Nancy boys!' someone called out.

'Supposed to be a chip off the old block,' another responded, creating a ripple of laughter.

That did it for Chip. Enraged, he came at Henry, who parried a right, then a left. But there was no let up as the right came again, under his defences this time, hit his stomach like a hammer, doubling him up. Swallowing a mouthful of bile, he staggered back, forced himself to straighten up. Chip went after him, firing two blows at his head, missing, but catching his ear with a third blow. Then, changing tactics, he kicked out viciously, aiming for his Henry's groin, but he was already dancing away. Henry risked a glance over the crowd, hoping the cavalry was on its way, but could see no sign.

Buoyed by the crowd's encouragement, Chip advanced. Henry ducked under a punch, jabbed at his jaw, connected and simultaneously brought his heel down hard on Chip's toes. Chip reeled backwards, neither blow enough to do much damage, but enough in them to dent his confidence. He started to circle again, probing rather than rushing.

Henry felt they'd been at it for an age. But he knew a second could feel like a minute in a fight; in reality probably only a couple of minutes had passed. Hopefully, before Chip gathered himself for his next all out onslaught, help would arrive.

It was a forlorn hope. Abandoning any pretence at a scientific approach, Chip rushed him, all guns blazing. Henry endured a battery of kicks and punches, which ended when he managed to get both arms around his opponent in a bear hug. Pushing his hair right into Chip's face, he rubbed hard, then released him and stepped away. Chip went straight after him but jerked to a halt, pawed at his face and eyes. The Fiery Jack Ointment Henry had rubbed into his hair back in the barn, a dirty trick but a necessary one, had done a job.

Chip stared at Henry through watery, red eyes. Like a

179

bear pawing itself, he rubbed his eyes again, cursing Henry who knew he was so enraged that next time he wouldn't stop until he'd used up all his formidable strength. He risked another glance over the crowd, thought he detected signs of movement near the door, didn't have time to let his gaze linger because Chip was starting forward now, a grim implacability about him that compelled full attention.

'Everybody stay exactly where you are!'

The booming voice echoed around the building, followed by a moment of perfect quiet, as though an hypnotic spell had been cast. Not immune to it, Chip froze, an uncomprehending look on his face. Henry let out a sigh of relief. He could see a detective standing near the door with a megaphone in his hands. Uniformed police were pouring into the building. This was what he'd been waiting for. Why had it taken so long?

The crowd came back to life. Heads swivelled seeking the voice's source. Then a low, angry murmur started, grew in impetus, reached a crescendo as armed police in riot gear swarmed the place.

Chip stared at the policemen dressed in riot gear who burst into the cage. A plain clothes detective followed them, looked the fighters up and down with a triumphant gleam in his eye.

'So you like playing in cages,' he said. 'Well, I'm sure we can provide one for you where you're going.'

Chip and the referee knew they were beaten, said nothing. Scowling, they did as they were told, headed out of the cage, Henry falling in behind them. The punters had formed a single file, were flanked by police all the way to the door. They'd been caught bang to rights at an illegal fight and their glum faces showed their displeasure. The Jacksons were off to one side surrounded by police. Henry couldn't see Frank with them.

A policeman at the door took names. From his lugubrious expression, he was bored with the task, but perked up when it was the turn of the two fighters who were given priority at the front of the queue.

'King Kong and Godzilla, is it?' he asked, brandishing his pen.

Chip grunted, 'Mister Chip Jackson to you, pig.'

Henry gave his name. Then they were taken outside into a blaze of floodlights. The yard was full of police vans, spectators climbing in, faces like undertakers.

They were ordered into one of the vans. Danny, Jet and Terry were already inside, huddled on a bench like three identical ornaments on a crowded mantelpiece. All three were staring fixedly into space, silent as the grave. Henry took a secret delight in their discomfiture. Like them, he was put in handcuffs. Finally, two armed policemen climbed inside. One of them closed the doors and the van drove off.

The miserable drone of the engine complemented the sombre mood of the men. Danny finally dragged his eyes in Henry's direction, stared hard, as though his brain was emerging from an enforced sleep, thinking dark thoughts.

'Where's that brother of yours, Torrance?'

Henry shrugged. He'd been wondering himself, figured he'd been lumped in with the punters, the money he'd been holding confiscated.

'There are other vans.'

Jet flicked his eyes at Henry. 'Someone's grassed us up!'

Henry understood what he was implying, but Terry threw his bit in just to make sure.

'Couldn't possibly be dear old Frank, could it?'

Chip rubbed his eyes with his sleeve, said inconsequentially, 'That bastard rubbed something in my eyes.'

Henry ignored him, concentrated on Danny. 'I'm not my brother's keeper.'

'Bastard was holding all the money,' Danny said.

Henry didn't like the way this was going, decided to nip it in the bud. 'If he's done something, it's without my knowledge. It's my money, too, not just yours.' He took a deep breath. 'Besides, like as not he'll be in another van.'

The rest of the journey passed in silence. Henry kept his head down, wishing he was somewhere else instead of being confined in this poky van with men he despised as human vermin. But he knew it was all for his own good, a charade for his own protection.

Half an hour later they stepped down into the courtyard at Middlesbrough Police Headquarters. The guards ushered them inside, into a large room where they sat in plastic chairs. A custody sergeant, with a world weary expression that said he was the veteran of a thousand such nights, was behind a desk out front.

Danny was first to be charged. Henry wondered about the other punters, presumed they'd been dispersed to different police stations, leaving this one to deal with the main players. But he'd told them Frank was a main player, so where was he? The Jacksons had voiced their suspicion and Frank's absence was disconcerting.

Two detectives in smart suits came into the room,

hovered near the desk. In contrast to the sergeant's insouciance, they seemed to give off an enthusiastic glow. As Danny Jackson was led out, he looked them up and down as though he was head of CID and they mere minions.

'You must be hard up for business,' he sniffed. 'All that trouble and we'll be out before you get your next paltry pay cheques.'

Jet heard and piped up, 'They must have done their quota of motorists this month. Got nothing better to do now than spoil people's fun.'

One of the detectives, who must have been close to fifty, smiled. 'You're on the canvas, boy. Don't think you'll beat the count either.'

Terry gave him the eyes. 'What's this, *Call My Bluff*?'

'No worries, lads,' Danny called out to his sons as he exited.

Henry saw the look pass between the brothers. They wouldn't do much time on account of an illegal fight and they knew it. The detective was all hot air.

Jet and Henry were the last to be processed. Jet was called up before Henry and, as he exited, glanced over his shoulder. His eyes narrowed until they were no more than slits. The strip lighting showed up dark semi-circles underneath, as though someone had used black crayon on them to make him look more evil.

'Let's hope Frank hasn't kippered us,' he said, 'or there'll be Hell to pay.'

Henry turned his head away. He didn't care a jot what happened to his brother or the money. He had a different agenda. All he cared about was returning to a normal life.

After the custody sergeant was finished with him, Henry was led into a long corridor with rows of cells. All the bad memories of his time in gaol came crowding in. He consoled himself with the thought that, if he could endure five years, one more night was a mere flea bite.

Inside his cell, he was given paper clothes. Once he'd changed the guards took his clothes and locked him in. But he was only alone for a few minutes before a young policeman entered the cell, accompanied by a short man who had a vague, distracted air as though his mind was somewhere else. Putting his bag on the bed, he announced brusquely that he was a doctor and needed to examine him for any damage done during the fight. Henry submitted himself to the examination and had his cuts and bruises treated. Job done, without so much as a nod in Henry's direction, the doc marched out with the guard on his heels. Henry wondered about the Hippocratic oath, if it included treating all men with common courtesy.

Surprisingly, Henry managed to get some sleep but awoke disorientated. He reached out, touched the wall, realized what he'd thought a grey mist was in fact solid and remembered where he was. He lay there wishing time away until finally the door unlocked and the young police constable from the night before stepped in carrying a plastic mug and two slices of toast on a plastic plate.

'Wife doesn't bring me tea in bed,' the constable mumbled. 'Must be bliss.'

Henry took the breakfast from him and grinned. 'Talking of bliss, how long are they going to keep me in this cave?'

'No idea,' the constable replied. 'Enjoy!'

The constable left and Henry took his time over the tea

and toast, eking it out. He didn't have a watch and it seemed like hours before the door opened again. It was the same fellow who'd brought his breakfast but with a pair of handcuffs this time. The custody sergeant was just a step behind him.

'We've got to handcuff you, son,' the sergeant told him. 'All right?'

It was nice to be asked, Henry thought, shrugging.

'I must be going on a trip.'

'Just to an interview room, son. Detectives Oates and Brownlee want to speak to you.'

Henry held his hands out. The sergeant took the cuffs from the constable and put them on Henry's wrists.

'Off you go, then. No trouble, eh!'

Henry smiled at the young constable who was looking a bit tentative.

'It's my legs you have to watch,' he announced in a stage whisper. 'I'm a cage fighter. They're deadly weapons, my legs.'

A worried look crossed the constable's face. The remark had been a reversion to an old habit from prison. Keep the screws on their toes. But he immediately regretted using it on the constable, realizing he was just a harmless rookie.

'Don't worry,' he said. 'I'm a gentle giant really, my granny's favourite.'

The interview room was as he'd expected, cold and functional. He figured it must have witnessed the whole range of human emotions in its time, yet its ambience remained devoid of soul. Henry had read somewhere that walls could absorb everything that occurred within a room, that future generations would use technology to extract past happenings from them, that walls truly would speak. If that was true, he figured these particular walls would be the greatest repository of human folly. Why weren't they weeping blood?

Two detectives were seated behind a table, shoulder to shoulder. The detective he knew as Oates, a tall, cadaverous man with an aquiline nose and swarthy complexion, gestured at the chair opposite.

Brownlee, the other detective, was smaller and rounder. He wore a dark jacket but his tie was bright red, like his cheeks. Henry thought the red seemed incongruous in this room, like the red coat the little girl wore in the film *Schindler's List*, the only splash of colour in depressing black and white scenes.

Henry sat and Oates leaned back. 'Hope you weren't treated too badly.'

'Water off a duck's back,' Henry told him. 'Served a purpose.'

Brownlee puffed out his cheeks out so that they were like red balloons.

'Served your purpose and our purpose. After the raid, we used the Jacksons' own Mercedes to approach Brass Farm. In the dark the guards assumed it was the family inside the car. We took the place by complete surprise. Apart from a large quantity of heroin we found a factory for growing cannabis.'

'Your photographs, plus the conversation you recorded on the mobile, will be a big help,' Oates added.

'Only the second time we've used that crafty little mobile,' Brownlee enthused. 'It's a fairly new invention.'

Henry grinned ruefully, pointed to his bruised cheeks.

'What took you so long? I was beginning to wonder, thought the thing hadn't worked.'

'Sorry about that.' Oates had the grace to look embarrassed. 'The technology was spot on but there was a bad road accident, held us up for a good few minutes.' He quickly changed the subject. 'But we're very grateful to you. We'll be able to put the Jacksons away for years. You did the right thing coming to us.'

Brownlee puffed out those florid cheeks. 'Just one little blip.'

Henry had a feeling he knew what was coming even before Oates elaborated.

'Frank – your brother – has disappeared into thin air. One of our lads found a hole in the wall at the back of the building just big enough to crawl through. We think he used it to slip away.'

Henry shook his head. He wasn't really surprised. Frank was always one for an escape route. He should have remembered that vulpine mind of his. While he was negotiating in the barn his brother had probably sniffed around, found that hole. He always did know how to take care of his own skin.

'We'll get him,' Oates said, thrusting his chin forward. 'And you could say he's done you a favour. His absence makes it look as though he was the one who came to us, not you.'

Henry placed his elbows on the table, eyed both of them in turn.

'When I'm safely out of Teesside, I'll have that kind of confidence.'

'All fixed,' Brownlee said, wafting a hand. 'You can leave

187

tomorrow. We've fixed up that house in Bournemouth we spoke about.'

'A change of names would be good,' Oates chipped in.

'I'll talk to the others,' Henry began. 'I don't think—'

A knock on the door stopped him mid-sentence. A thick-set detective entered and approached the desk. He leaned between Oates and Brownlee. Henry couldn't catch what he was saying, but surmised, from the way all three kept glancing in his direction, he featured in the exchange in a big way.

Finally, heads nodding in agreement, the trio broke apart. The newcomer plodded to the door. Henry noticed Brownlee and Oates exchange quick glances, sensed their hesitancy. Neither seemed to want to take the lead now and he had the idea it couldn't be good news. When they did speak, they started up simultaneously, had to rein themselves in. Finally, Oates took the initative, placed his hand on Brownlee's arm and spoke out.

'Your father collapsed last night in his caravan. They think it was his heart. They've taken him to hospital. We're arranging a car to take you straight there.'

It took a moment to sink in. The old man wasn't well, but he still thought of him as indestructible. He was tempted to tell the detective not to bother with the car; he wasn't going to the hospital. After all that had happened in the past, why should he go? They'd probably have nothing to say to each other.

'There's something else,' Oates said.

'You've caught Frank,' Henry mumbled, not fully concentrating.

'No, not that. It's a delicate matter, Henry.' He paused

thoughtfully, as though working out the best way to say it.
'In hospital, your father called for a policeman and made a
confession. He's requested to be allowed to tell you about
it rather than you hearing it from us. The way he is – well,
it could be his last request.'

Henry nodded, supposed he'd have to go. As Father
Andrew had kept telling him, ultimately he was his father,
no matter what. Blood was thicker than water. Had Frank
heard that one?

'I'm ready to go,' he said.

Fred Torrance was in a small room on his own when Henry
walked in. He was propped up on pillows, face chalk
white, thinner even than the last time he'd spoken to him.
His eyes were closed and he had a peaceful look as though
a weight he'd been carrying for years had suddenly
dropped off his shoulders and nothing mattered quite as
much any more.

Henry pulled up a chair, wondering whether his father
would wake. But as soon as he sat down, he opened his
eyes as though he had sensed his arrival, raised his arm,
and pointed it at Henry's face.

'Bruises!'

Henry felt sympathy for the old man. He looked so
pitiful. Like Tom Daly, his father had never enjoyed being
shut in, and this was a small room for a gypsy who had
once roamed. Yet, he needed to be here, needed to be taken
care of. If his time had come, it was better than dying alone
and uncared for in his caravan.

'He could punch,' Henry said.

'But you won, didn't you?'

Henry knew what his father wanted to hear, how much
it meant to him to hear it. It was all there in his eyes, even
as death stalked him. What harm now to give him what he
wanted?

'Yeah, sure. I won – for the Torrance name.'

A ghost of a smile flitted across the old man's face.
'Knew you would.' He closed his eyes as a spasm of pain
hit him, opened them again when it passed. 'And Frank?
What about him?'

'Free of debt now.' It was a straight lie but what was the
harm. 'A fresh start, if he takes it.'

With a look like thunder, Fred Torrance shook his head.
'Too late for him.'

Henry didn't understand. Did his father know about
Frank disappearing, that he was being hunted? How could
he?

'Nothing for you to worry about. Everything's cushty.'

His father opened his eyes wide, looked right through
him.

'I've told the police everything – last confession.'
Grimacing, he added, 'You need to hear it.'

What did he mean, Henry wondered? That he'd told
them about Frank's drug dealing? If that was so, why then
had the detectives implied it was such a delicate matter
when he'd already informed them about his brother's
activities himself?

Henry forced a smile. 'Last confession? Don't think so!
There's plenty of sinning left in you.'

Fred's eyes twinkled for a moment, then his face took on
a grave look.

'We both know there won't be time for that. I've been a

sinner, Henry, God forgive me.' He lowered his head until his chin almost touched his chest. 'But you don't know the worst of it. Not yet.'

Henry was perplexed. Seeing his father enfeebled, he wondered again how he could have stored so much hate for him. But it was true he had never been a good father since their mother died, thought more of the booze than anything else. Then, when he'd needed him most, he'd abandoned him so callously. Nothing could excuse that. It would always be there, niggling.

Fred Torrance lifted his chin, looked at him sideways, seemed to sense what he was thinking.

'Your mother – she kept me on the straight and narrow. When she died—' A paroxysm of coughing shook his body.

Henry poured a glass of water from the jug on the side cabinet, put it to his father's lips.

'Take it easy,' he told him.

As he removed the glass, his father grabbed his arm, dug his fingers into his flesh.

'You're going to hate me even more,' he said, tears starting to roll down his cheeks. 'I've tried to put it right but you're going to hate me in my grave.'

Henry saw the haunted look on his face. It was clear he was suffering mental as well as physical trauma, that his conscience was extracting a horrible revenge at the end.

'Don't worry,' Henry said, taking no pleasure from his suffering. 'There isn't much can hurt me any more.'

'Difficult,' Fred groaned. 'So difficult.'

His father's hand gripped his. He could feel that flesh from which he had sprung cold as ice against his own. Was this a last chance for his father to purge his demons as the grim reaper looked on, axe raised to sever his earthly ties? Was he to act as his reluctant confessor?

'Don't worry. Just tell me.'

The words seemed to give the old man a measure of reassurance. He raised his head, focused on his son, but behind his eyes his brain seemed to be replaying a memory, compelling and repulsing him simultaneously.

'Frank,' he hissed, from wherever his mind had taken him. 'He was the reason.'

The venom in the voice surprised Henry.

'Take it easy,' he said again.

His father's eyes bulged in their sockets, his fingers dug deeper into Henry's flesh.

'Have to tell you,' he said.

He flopped back on the pillow, let out a sigh, suddenly spoke out, his words stronger and clearer, like a judge's final summation from the bench.

'Frank – your brother – he killed Bull Jackson. Not you, Henry.'

Henry's head jerked upright. What was this? The old man's mind had surely given up on him, confusing the events of the past. Could he be hallucinating?

'Frank didn't,' Henry said, pitying him.

'Listen to me! The police know it was him. I told them.'

Henry couldn't take it in. The old man seemed to be all there and the detective had mentioned a confession, something his father wanted to tell him face to face. But what he'd just heard was crazy. How could it possibly be?

'We were running from the police, Frank and me,' his father continued. 'I saw Bull staggering in the field, weak as water from the fight – then I saw Frank.' He paused.

Tears started to run down his cheeks and he put his hands over his face. 'I've had to live with it all these years,' he groaned.

Henry waited, wondering what was coming next. Then, with an evident effort of will, the old man uncovered his face, wiped away those tears and focused on his son.

'Frank didn't hesitate. He came up behind Bull, struck three hard blows to his head. Bull sank to his knees unconscious. Frank doesn't know to this day I saw him do it.'

Henry stared at his father, his body rigid with shock. He couldn't believe what he'd just heard. If it was true, he'd been down a bad road, all for nothing. But why should the old man lie on his death bed? It had to be true. He sat in silence, not looking at his father as he struggled to come to terms with the magnitude of what he had just heard, fighting his fury at the injustice of it. When he finally found his voice, it spilled over with bitterness.

'Why didn't you tell the police at the time? Why did you protect him, not me?'

'The Jacksons would have killed him or had him killed. He was still my son.'

'So I had to suffer for him?'

His father's sigh was the cry of a wind lost in a desolate canyon in a far off mountain, a world of sorrow in it.

'The Jacksons wouldn't touch you for something that they thought happened during a fair fight. That's the way it's always been. The whole gypsy community would have known about it and it would have shamed them, especially in fight circles.'

'So it didn't matter that I had to go to prison?'

'I thought you could take prison. You had your mother's mental strength.' He couldn't look at Henry and his voice dropped to a whisper. 'It was a terrible choice – the wrong choice.'

Henry felt numb. Five years in a hell hole, guilt about killing a man tormenting his soul, bringing him to the brink of suicide, all for nothing. His father was suffering now but he'd had it far worse. He fought hard to batten his fury down. What good would it do? His father was punishing himself anyway.

'You never visited me.' His words seemed inconsequential, pathetic after what he had just heard.

'God forgive me, I should have, but I couldn't bear the thought, knowing what I knew. Would have cracked me up, son. Should have put it right, but once the ball was rolling – there was no going back.'

'Why?' Henry said. 'Why did he strike Bull down?'

'Jealousy. Bull's wife was once Frank's girl, gave him up for Bull. Must have brooded on it, saw his chance. He acted like a . . . coward . . . not a Torrance.'

'And the police know all this?'

Fred nodded. He looked exhausted. The effort and emotion involved in telling his tale had been too much for him.

'Need your forgiveness, son,' he gasped. 'Don't deserve it.'

A welter of emotions washed around Henry's brain, but one fact fought its way to the surface. Father Andrew had spoken about the virtues of forgiveness, how it healed a man's soul. This was his father pleading with him. How could he turn his back and live with it afterwards? Though it didn't come easily, he reached out, placed his hand gently on his father's shoulder, spoke as softly as he could manage.

'You did what you thought was right to protect your son. I can understand that. There's nothing to forgive.' He forced a grin. 'Besides, prison did me a lot of good. Taking a long view, it was for the best, so rest easy.'

The tension at the corners of the old man's eyes vanished. His face regained that calmer look that had been there when Henry first entered. He sank further into the pillow, his white face seeming to merge with it. Henry could see he had very little energy left.

'Wanted you to understand,' he said, forcing the words. 'Want you to have a good life. Make up for—'

He was too tired to finish the sentence and drifted off to sleep, but Henry understood the sentiment, was moved by it.

Two hours later his father drew his last breath peacefully in his sleep. Henry was still at his bedside. He said his last goodbye, called for a nurse and walked out in a daze.

As though on autopilot, he negotiated the labyrinth of corridors to the exit and stepped out into the air. In his final hour, his father had freed them both from the chains of the past. Henry looked up at the stars and said a silent prayer to see him on his way in peace.

Late afternoon Henry knocked on the door of Mary's flat. After the hospital, he'd spent some time with the detectives finalizing things. Now he felt tired. When Mary opened up, he forced a grin but it didn't compensate enough for the melancholy look in his eye, nor the weary set to his shoulders. She noticed and her face creased with anxiety.

'Something's gone wrong?' she said, with a sharp intake of breath.He shook his head, reassured her everything had gone well and she shouldn't worry.

But she knew there was something. She reached out, touched the bruises on his face. Her gesture made him feel like a small boy again. Then, taking his hand, she led him into the kitchen, made him sit down.

'What is it? Tell me!'

He told her everything, from the moment Frank had picked him up, to his father's death in the hospital, how that had affected him more than he ever thought it would. Then came the final devastating revelation that he had served five years for something his brother had done, his father's complicity in the matter and his reasons for it. Mary was stunned, her eyes reflecting a myriad emotions as the long-buried secret unravelled. Finally, understanding no words could be enough, she put her arms around him and held him tight.

Eventually, he eased himself out of her arms. He knew he had to be practical; there were things he had to do, the quicker the better.

'It's Bournemouth for us now,' he said, forcing a smile. 'The police have it all organized.'

'Good! No slag heaps down there,' she said, smiling back at him,' and plenty of – what do they call it – sun?'

'Couldn't get much further away from the Jacksons and their brood,' he added. 'No chance they can wreak their vengeance, if by an unlucky chance they find out I grassed – maybe we'll change our names as well.'

A silence descended. The clock on the wall seemed to tick louder.

'You hated doing it, didn't you?' Mary said.

Henry sighed. 'Went against the grain. But the Jacksons had gone too far, didn't give a damn who they hurt. Gypsies have had to do all sorts to survive in the past, but they've never been big on drug dealing.'

'What about your brother? How do you feel about him?'

Henry made a face, as though he'd just swallowed a mouthful of foul tasting medicine.

'I hope he gets what he deserves.'

Mary nodded. 'Let's hope the police catch him.'

They wandered through to the living room, found John snoozing in an armchair.

'He was worried about you,' Mary said as she shook him awake.

'Bournemouth, kiddo!' Henry announced. 'Pack your bucket and spade.'

John's grin was broad enough to put a Cheshire cat to shame. Henry squeezed Mary's hand, letting her know he was grateful she'd agreed the lad could go with them. Once they were settled, they'd help him get his own place, keep a watchful eye on his welfare. Henry knew what it was like when your world spun off its axis. He hoped to do for the lad what others had done for him.

'My bags are packed,' Mary announced.

'So are mine. They're in the hallway at home just ready to pick up.' He glanced at John. 'I've some books in the house, some of them for you. Maybe you could come and pick out those you want.'

John put his coat on and Mary handed Henry her car

keys. 'Don't linger,' she said. 'The sooner we're gone the happier I'll feel.'

Henry drove while John, obviously excited at the prospect of the new start, chatted away ten to the dozen. But when they reached the outskirts of South Bank there was a change in his demeanour. Henry noticed he was quiet, watching the streets, eyes darting everywhere. He figured the lad was remembering the past, good memories of his time with his mother filtering through. Had it suddenly hit him he was leaving everything he'd known, wondering whether he could cope?

Henry said,' Sometimes it's hard to leave a place. That first step—'

'My mother would want me to leave, to better myself.' John interrupted. 'Right now I'm just keeping an eye out for Tonks. Know what I'd like to do to him.'

Henry heard the venom in the youth's voice. He'd have been the same at his age, angry in the face of perceived injustices, wanting the perpetrators to suffer, willing to act himself.

'Let it go, John!'

John's eyes darted in his direction. 'I haven't forgotten those horses – and other things. Why should he get off free?'

'You may think people like him get away with it,' Henry told him, 'but the consequences wait down the line for them, even years later.'

John frowned. 'You really believe that?'

'Seen it happen. Spent five years watching it happen to men around me, one way or another.' He thought about his own father, the burden he'd carried. 'Tonks will create his own Hell. Just see that you're not involved.'

*

Henry pulled into the kerb. His house had memories for him and he wouldn't forget his aunt's kindness. The police would arrange for it to be sold, pass the money on, but he didn't expect to get much for it.

'You go upstairs,' he told John, as he opened the door. 'The books I want are in the box but look through the shelves, pick out ones you fancy. Take your time. I'll make us a brew and call you when I'm ready.'

Henry's bags were packed and standing in the hall. They stepped around them and John started up the stairs. As he entered the living room, Henry remembered his benevolent aunt had been a tea jenny, strictly non-alcoholic, so he'd make a last, silent toast to her in the way she would have approved.

The door swung shut behind him and for a second he thought a ghost had taken up residence, was staring at him from the chair beside the fireplace. But it was no ghost. It was his brother Frank sitting there in the flesh, the gun in his hand all too real. His face had a weary, haunted look, red-rimmed eyes emanating malevolence.

'Come into my parlour, said the spider to the fly,' he hissed.

Henry's brain raced. Did Frank know he'd turned them in? The gun and that hateful look in his eyes suggested he did.

'Thought you'd got away,' Henry said, trying to keep his voice calm.

'Don't play games with a master,' Frank snapped back. 'With you in the clink, I thought I'd hide here. Then I see

199

PETER TAYLOR

the bags in the hall, know you're ready to run and wonder why.' He shook his head. 'Never thought grassing was your style.'

'It gave me pleasure, Frank, especially since the Jacksons blame you.' He saw a glimmer of fear in his brother's eyes. 'It never rains but it pours, eh, Frank?'

'I could always get the money back to the Jacksons, say I was protecting it – bring it all back to you. How'd you like that?'

'Wouldn't work. Sometime's there's one sin too many to hide.'

Frank's top lip lifted in a sneer. 'You were locked up too long, kidda. It addled your brain.'

Knowing what he knew, those words, that supercilious sneer, went in like a sword. His brother had no conscience about what he'd done to him.

'Nothing will help you now, Frank, because soon everybody's going to know the whole truth, see you for what you are.'

A shadow of doubt stole across his brother's face. Henry's moment had come. Payback for five long years. He couldn't keep the relish out of his voice.

'Yes, Brother, the police know you killed Bull. Struck him down like the coward you are.'

Frank's eyes narrowed to slits, his lips protruded. His defences had been pierced and it showed. He shifted the gun, the temptation to use it palpable.

'You're talking about the wrong brother, aren't you?'

Henry shook his head. 'The game's up, Frank. The police have it from a man who knows.'

Behind the cold blue eyes, he could see Frank's mind

working frantically, trying to work it out. Who could have witnessed his brutal, vengeful act in that fateful field, in the black of night, more than five years ago?

'Someone's been making mischief,' he said, squaring his shoulders, resisting it to the end. 'They're lying. It won't hold up.'

Henry spoke with slow deliberation, each word emphatic, like a slow drum roll.

'Your father's dying words will hold up.'

Frank neck seemed to shrink down into his shoulders. He just stared at Henry, making no more attempts at denial. The past had come back to him with a vengeance.

'What was it with you, Frank?'

His brother made a noise halfway between a snort and grunt.

'You were always the favourite, weren't you? Boxing! It was the only thing that counted with the old man. You were our mother's favourite too. When you came along, she couldn't see me for you.'

'The green-eyed monster!' Henry paused. 'For God's sake, I was a lot younger than you. That's why my mother paid me attention. As for our father, well, he chose to send me to prison to protect you. Don't kid yourself that's what turned you into a murderer, a drug dealer and all round sleaze bag. That's just pathetic.'

'How would you know anything?'

'Five years in prison taught me most men have a spark of decency but there are some just pure evil – psychopaths like you. They walk amongst us in the guise of humans but aren't like us. Maybe it's down to genes, I don't know. Walk in another man's shoes and you might understand

201

why he is what he is. But not with that kind – not you, Frank. Look at you. Not a spark of emotion when I mentioned the old man dying and he protected you all these years.'

'They'll never put me inside a prison,' Frank muttered, a wild look in his eyes.

'You're finished, Frank. Inside prison somebody will kill you. Outside, you'd better keep running.'

Frank showed his teeth in an animal snarl. 'Don't think you're going to come out of this smiling. Don't think I'm going to let you live after what you've done to me.'

Henry's stomach knotted. He had no doubt he meant it. Frank never made idle threats. Any moment now he'd have to rush him, take his chances, because the talking was just about done. Since he'd come into the room he'd been worried John would appear, could only hope the lad had heard them and got clear.

Frank pointed to the bag lying at his feet. Henry had seen it, knew what it contained.

'I'm set up for life, kidda. Guess you're one of those who have no luck in life. Or maybe it's just the genes. Maybe I got the lucky ones.'

Henry tensed. His throat constricted. After all the talking was done, what Frank said was true. He still had the upper hand.

A rap on the door raked the silence. Frank stared at it as though it was a portal to another world, one he'd temporarily forgotten existed outside the room. Henry feared it must be John, knocking out of politeness, believing he had a visitor. He opened his mouth to warn him but Frank pre-empted him.

'Come on in!'

The door swung open. John entered backwards, pushing it with his hip. He was holding a pile of books stacked right up to his chin. Turning, he saw Frank with the gun and his eyes widened.

'What's this?' he stammered, almost overbalancing.

Frank snapped, 'Keep still, damn you!'

'Let him go,' Henry said. 'He's done nothing to you!'

Franks eyes blazed like hot coals. 'He'll set the filth on my trail. Might as well make it two for the high road.'

John moved a fraction, bringing him closer to Henry. Henry felt acid bite into his gullet, bile rising up into his mouth. He knew Frank had made up his mind and nothing would divert him from killing them. He had to make his move, now or never.

Before he had a chance, John sprang forward, launched the books straight at Frank. They descended on him like a flock of angry birds and he tried to knock them away, flapping at them with both hands.

Henry seized his chance, rushed him. He made a grab for the gun barrel, twisting and pulling until it came free and the weapon fell to the floor. Then he struck Frank on the jaw. Stunned, his brother rocked backwards and was still.

Henry bent down, picked up the gun, stepped back until he was beside John who was gawping at Frank slouched in the chair.

'Never could take a punch,' Henry said.

'I heard voices,' John told him. 'I came downstairs, went out the back, peeped in the window, saw the gun, had to do something.'

Henry put an arm around his shoulder. 'Good job you did. He was getting ready to kill me.'

A groan came from the chair. Frank was starting to come round. His head was swaying like a drunk's, eyes blinking in an attempt to focus.

John said, 'Are you going to call the police?'

Henry hesitated. If the positions were reversed, he knew Frank wouldn't have any mercy. But he wasn't Frank. Stepping forward, he picked up the bag.

His brother was back in the world again now, was watching him as he stooped.

'Everything ready to go, John?'

John didn't answer, looked puzzled.

'You're not going to kill him, are you?'

Henry smiled. 'Like I told you before, his kind dig their own graves.' His gaze shifted to his brother. 'Go on, get out of here. Start running. Find a life – if you can.'

Frank stared at him, disbelieving. With his movements as stiff as an old man's, he levered himself out of the chair. Henry moved aside to let him pass. When he was at the door, he turned around. His eyes moved from Henry's face to the bag in his hand.

'Gonna keep all that money for yourself?' he asked hoarsely, a weary resignation in his voice.

'My business!'

Frank nodded.

'I was wrong before. You were always the lucky one!'

With that, he turned and walked through the door. Henry followed, watched him walk down the street. For a moment, he thought he could see his father when he was young, that same walk, that same shape to the shoulders.

Then, before he turned the corner Frank stopped, looked back. This time Henry caught a glimpse of himself, like a reflection in a far off mirror. It sent a shiver down his spine. Then his brother was gone, leaving him sad for what might have been.

They were driving away from the house, each lost in his own thoughts. Henry glanced at John, was pleased to see that the colour had returned to his face. He could feel his own spirits lifting, a glimmer of optimism burgeoning.

'One last visit to make,' he told John. 'Then we'll collect Mary and start heading south before my brother can find any new tricks. You can never be sure with him.'

He parked outside the Community Hall, reached onto the back seat for the bag. Telling John to wait in the car because he needed to do this alone, he stepped out and entered the building. He couldn't spot Micky in the main hall so, walking past the lads who were hard at it on the exercise machines, he headed for the kitchen.

Micky was at the sink, his back to him. He had his sleeves rolled up and he was up to his elbows in soapy water. Henry smiled at the image; it wasn't one he associated with his old trainer. He felt a sudden surge of affection, mingled with respect. After a bad start, Mick had conquered his demons, given the lie to those who said a leopard couldn't change its spots, his work here a testament to that.

'Is it you, or your ghost come to haunt me?' Micky's gravelly voice cut into the silence.

Henry laughed. Age hadn't diminished Micky's awareness.

205

'The Devil wasn't ready for me. Told me to come and tap you on the shoulder.'

Mick faced him, soap suds dripping from his arms onto the floor. Henry had made him aware of all his plans, had been anxious for his approval.

'So you survived.'

Henry nodded. 'It wasn't as straightforward as that.'

He told Micky everything. The trainer's facial expressions reflected a range of emotions, settled on anger at the injustice of Henry's prison sentence. When the anger passed from his face, there was something akin to admiration in his eyes.

'So you didn't strain the quality of mercy, letting your brother go like that?'

'It certainly didn't drop like gentle rain from heaven – more like a deluge after thunder. Anyway Frank won't last long the way he is, so it doesn't matter.'

Mick nodded. His expression grew suddenly grave, as though he'd just remembered something that worried him.

'Shouldn't you get going, son? The plan was to get out of Teesside, wasn't it?'

Henry looked through the hatch into the hall. All the lads were occupied so he lifted the bag, unzipped it and scooped half the bundles of money onto the table.

Mick's frown emphasized the furrows on his forehead. He rubbed his chin speculatively, eyes flitting between Henry and the money.

'You ain't robbed a bank, have you?'

'It's the prize money. I took it from Frank. That's my share. I want you to use it for this place.'

Micky rubbed the back of his neck, stared at the money

as though he didn't know what to say, couldn't quite believe it.

Finally, he said, 'It's your money. I can't take your money.'

'It's what I want, Micky.'

The old trainer picked up a towel, dried his arms.

'You'll need it, son. Wherever you're going – you'll need it.'

Henry held up the bag. 'There's more than enough left here to see me through. Besides, there could be compensation for serving time.' He fixed his eyes on Micky's. 'Let me do this!'

Micky rolled down his sleeves absent-mindedly. Sounds drifted in from the hall, lads hard at work on the machines, fists rapping out a rhythm on the punch bags.

'We need money,' he said, 'can't deny it.'

Henry waited, hoping. When Mick spoke again, there was a throb in his throat, barely contained emotion in his voice.

'Every penny will be spent wisely – to keep the place going.'

Henry let out a sigh, laid a hand on his shoulder. 'Don't justify anything to me, Micky. I know what you'll do with it.'

Henry started for the door. 'You can come for a holiday when things settle. Plenty of rich widows where we're going, looking for a toy boy like you.'

Micky grimaced. 'Get out of here, kidda, or I'll give you one last lesson in that ring.'

Henry laughed, with a last wave retreated through the door. He hoped he'd see Micky again. If fate decreed otherwise, he knew he'd always remember him, the way he'd tried to help him, his loyalty. Giving him half that money had been the least he could do. You should never forget.

On their way back to Mary, he stopped at a lonely spot beside the River Tees. Leaving John in the car, he walked a short distance along the bank, then took Frank's gun from his pocket and cast it a short distance into the water, with a sense of relief watched the ripples it made die away.

Frank Torrance checked to see the lugubrious landlord wasn't looking, popped another amphetamine pill into his mouth and slurped it down with a swig of beer from his pint glass. Hopefully the combination would lift him out of the depression that he could feel coming, as it had so often these last three months since he'd fled Middlesbrough.

He caught his reflection in the mirror behind the bar, quickly looked away, but had already seen enough to disturb him. His eyes looked dark and sunken, his cheekbones hollowed like one of those junkies he'd lived off in Middlesbrough in what seemed another lifetime now. He knew it was the way he'd been living ; a bed-sit in the worst part of Sunderland, cheap food, constantly looking over his shoulder. None of it did anything for his health. The little money he'd scraped together before he'd left town in a hurry was almost gone.

He'd chosen this pub down near the river because it was out of the mainstream. There was only a handful of drinkers in, mostly old men who looked like they'd been part of the furniture for years and a man and a woman absorbed in a game of darts. Not much danger any of them could be connected with the gypsy community, not like last night when he'd risked a city centre pub and thought he saw a familiar face staring at him in recognition through the crowd of drinkers. With hindsight, he figured it was probably his own paranoia, the constant awareness that the Jacksons would have the word out, promising money to whoever saw him and reported back. Even in prison they could reach out.

He took a tiny mouthful of beer, intending to make it last. One way out would be to pull off a big job, country mansion or something. That would give him the wherewithal to leave the country, settle somewhere in the sun where there'd be far less chance of being recognized. Maybe a touch of cosmetic surgery would help. Trouble was he'd have to do the job alone, couldn't afford to contact any of his erstwhile partners because they were all gypsies and he couldn't be sure they wouldn't betray him.

His glass was well down when he heard the door open, felt a wind caress the hair on the back of his neck. He turned around, watched a woman walk in and settle at the other end of the bar. She was a smart piece of work, this one, coal black hair, alabaster skin offset by full red lips, well dressed too, a bit too classily for this place. After the barman served her a whisky and soda, she turned her head briefly in his direction and he thought he saw a ghost of a smile that was meant for him. Then she made her way to a corner table and sat down.

Her smile lingered with him, though, intriguing, like the smile of an old, long lost lover you think has faded from memory with the passage of the years; he was nearly certain it was a come on. After all, she was a woman alone and not many of her sex would have had the bottle to enter a bar alone with all that poise and assurance she'd carried with her. He tried to figure it but gave up, dismissing the idea that he could have seen her before; a woman like that he would have remembered.

It took him another pint and another amphetamine to find his courage. Then he crossed the room to her table, looked down at her and took the direct approach.

'Need company?'

She gave him that smile again. 'Took you long enough. Thought I was going to have to come to the bar, chat you up.'

Visibly preening, he lowered himself into the chair facing her. Perhaps his luck was on the turn at last. It had been a long time since he'd been in a woman's company and this one was prime stock.

The conversation started to flow and, as the night wore on, he forgot his troubles, felt more and more like his old self. The best of it was, unlike most of the women he'd picked up, she didn't enquire into his past and let him do the best part of the talking. He felt in control and that was how he liked it.

At closing time she did another thing he liked. Tilting her head coquettishly, she took the initiative.

'Have you got a car?'

He patted his belly. 'Walked! Better for the figure.'

'We'll need a taxi, then.' She ran her fingers down her sides. 'My figure's good enough.'

He laughed out loud, not missing the fact she'd said 'we'll' need, not 'I'll', and he wasn't going to disagree with that. It seemed an age since he'd enjoyed himself like this.

It was as though she'd known him all her life, was attuned to his thoughts. But now he had a problem. He couldn't ask her back to that stinking bed sit, could he? Once again, as though this was the night his fortune was about to change, she solved his problem for him.

'It'll have to be my place for – coffee. My sister rings every night around midnight, worries if I'm not in and haven't told her.'

'Fine,' he said. 'Ready when you are.'

She used her mobile to ring for the taxi. As soon as they stepped outside, it loomed out of the darkness. The driver was out and had the doors open in no time. Frank fell into the back, so close to her now he could smell her perfume. It added to her allure and he wished he could bathe in it forever. He draped an arm around her as she gave the driver an address which he knew was in the best part of the town.

'Bet you've got a nice place,' he said,' a woman like you.' He was thinking maybe if he played his cards right he could get his feet under the table, hide out with her in comfort for a while.

She gave him that smile he found so enigmatic. 'You'll be surprised.'

He grinned. 'Good! I like to be surprised.'

Frank could see lights reflecting off the dark ribbon of the River Wear. So close it seemed almost directly overhead, one of the bridges reached across the water, a giant bicep silhouetted against the skyline. The taxi was bouncing over pothole riddled roads, past disused warehouses, going towards the water. Even in his half intoxicated state, he was aware there were no houses, no major roads in that direction.

He was on the point of saying something when they entered a tunnel and the taxi jerked to a halt. Its headlights extinguished and the interior lights came on. Frank sat forward, confused.

'What's happening?'

The driver turned around. His upper lip curled into a sneer as he looked directly at him with a knowing look. Warning bells sounded in Frank's head but, before he could speak or move, the door on his side opened, strong arms reached in, hauled him out of the taxi as though he weighed no more than a bag of shopping. He landed on his back in the road. Looking up, he saw the woman was leaning out of the car, looking down on him, not moving to help. Half of her face was in shadow and he could only see the part that was lit by the interior light, yet he could have sworn she was smiling. Then someone put a sack over his head. In total darkness, he was hauled to his feet.

He tried to resist, but it was only a token effort and his arms were soon pinioned against his sides, rope wound around his torso until he was trussed up like a chicken ready for the oven. His attackers bundled him back into the car. He started to wriggle but this time a fist struck the side of his head and he knew there'd be more of the same if he persisted. Bodies with muscles that felt like iron sat either side of him, wedged him in like a thin piece of meat between two hunks of bread.

He tried to calm himself but his brain was a scattergun, firing questions he didn't want to hear because he was afraid of the answers. The big question, the one that was screaming at him above the others, was whether this had to do with the Jacksons. Logic answered that it must. Why else would this be happening?

He heard the taxi draw to a halt. The men got out, hauled him after them. Though he knew it was futile with that sack over his head, his fear got the better of him and he tried to break away, make a run for it. All he received for his trouble was another blow on his jaw and this time he went out like a light.

They'd caught a good day to visit the New Forest and Henry wasn't disappointed. He felt carefree, like those times as a gypsy boy he'd travelled the old country roads. Patches of blue sky showed through the canopy of trees overhead and the sun was shimmering in the branches. He'd come here because he remembered Tom Daly talking about the New Forest, his eyes lighting up that sombre prison cell when he'd spoken about the ponies roaming free there. That seemed an age ago, but when he caught the briefest glimpse of four ponies galloping through the trees like ghosts, manes streaming behind them, he said a silent prayer for Tom, hoped his spirit was as free as those ponies.

Glancing at Mary beside him, he considered himself a lucky man to have a woman who'd given up everything to be with him. They'd been in Bournemouth three months now and were happy. John had settled well, was attending college. He was with them today in the back seat, staring out the window. Apart from his trips to the horse sanctuary, the lad had rarely left South Bank. Henry could imagine the forest would be like another world to him. He was glad the lad had taken his advice, written to his father telling him he was going away, wishing him luck. You had to leave doors open. Things and people changed – sometimes.

The headache came on that night just before he went to bed, a bad end to what had been a perfect day. He hadn't had a drink, couldn't think of anything he'd eaten that could have caused it. Perhaps he'd driven a little further than usual but driving didn't usually affect him. He mentioned it to Mary who told him to take two aspirins and go to bed, have a lie in next day.

Frank felt the cold seeping into his bones, thought he was in his damp bed-sit. As his eyes fluttered open, he was expecting to see the light of a new day peeping through the holes in the curtains, was surprised when there was nothing but blackness. He was puzzled because it had a different quality from the black that comes with the night, was all consuming, not a shadow or a glimmer of light sneaking through, more like the blackness of the grave. He became aware of something rough like the coarse hair of an animal rubbing against his face. Then his fear uncoiled and struck, feeding his imagination. He tried frantically to wriggle away, found he couldn't move a muscle, thought he was paralysed. Finally, he remembered, but it didn't help.

'He's awake,' an Irish voice called from a distance. 'Twitching like a chicken without a head, so he is.'

Footsteps echoed on concrete. They halted close to him.

'Fetch them,' another Irish voice commanded. 'It's time.'

Frank wanted to cry out, beg. What stopped him was an

adamantine quality he'd detected in those voices, a hint of mercilessness that, by a process of osmosis he understood well, because he possessed it himself.

Now he heard more footsteps, including what he thought was the click of high heels, surmised those belonged to the woman. What part had she in this? What was it about her that had intrigued him? What had he failed to decipher?

Rough hands untied the rope around his chest and the sack was pulled upwards. Light exploded all around him, blinding him for a second. When his eyes adjusted he realized he was in a warehouse, bright strip lighting overhead. He was bound to a metal chair and four figures were lined up watching him like members of a firing squad, their accusing eyes deadly weapons. The woman was standing next to a boy who couldn't have been more than ten years old. Two burly males flanked them, staring at Frank with contempt. The faces of the woman and the boy were way beyond contempt, brimful with hatred for him, as though it wouldn't take much for them to tear him to pieces with their bare hands. He understood then that nothing he could say would move them. The woman had the mad look of a she-devil incarnate.

'Why? he asked, his voice strangulated, hoping against hope that he was wrong, that there was a way out for him.

'Justice!'

The word snapped from those luscious, blood red lips like the crack of doom – his doom.

She came forward, kneeled down in front of him like an acolyte at the feet of a holy man, except there was not a hint of rapture in her fierce expression.

'Who are you?' he asked.

Reaching into her pocket, she pulled out a handkerchief, wiped away her lipstick, rubbed those alabaster cheeks. When her make up was off, he noticed little brown spots on her cheeks, realized they were freckles, which seemed incongruous with that dark hair. She looked up at him.

'Know me now!'

Her tone was so different from the tone she'd used in the pub. It was as though the last person in the world she wanted to speak to was him and she was having to force her words through a strainer.

He stared hard, trying to place her. That smile, the one that had flirted with his memory, must have been a clue he'd been foolish to ignore. Realizing he still didn't know her, she put her hand to her brow, lifted the black hair right back so that he saw fair roots beneath the black.

The way it takes time to see the meaning in an abstract painting and then you wonder why you hadn't seen it earlier, the woman's face metamorphosed before his eyes into that of a fresh-faced sixteen-year-old girl. Under-standing made him jerk his head backwards away from her, emptied him of any hope. Now, he knew. Now, he got the who and the why.

She saw it all happening to him, relished it, smiled her satisfaction.

'It was jealousy, wasn't it?' she hissed. 'Just because I turned you down for a better man – for Bull.'

Frank nodded. He knew it was no good lying to her. Nothing mattered now. He was done for.

'I would never have married you,' she said. 'But I never told Bull how you pursued me like an idiot, turned nasty

216

after I turned you down.' Her voice rose. 'I tried to protect you and look what you did to my Bull, you – filth.'

He lowered his head but she was tenacious, hadn't finished with him, scourged him with her voice.

'Look at the lad!'

When he didn't obey, she grabbed his hair, lifted his head.

The boy was looking at him with a steady gaze. There was no innocence in his eyes.

'That's Bull's son. The lad you deprived of a father. He's had to grow up fast has Charlie, too fast, had to be man when he was still a child – all because of you.'

She let go of his hair, addressed the two men.

'Let him see!'

They dragged the chair backwards, the scraping noise on the concrete like a scream tearing at his fractured nerves. The men bent down beside him. He heard other scraping sounds, metal sliding against metal, realized they were bolting the chair into the ground.

One of the men stood in front of him, pointed skyward. Frank looked up. Five feet above his head, there was a steel block the size of a washing machine suspended from a gangway that ran across the warehouse. It didn't take much imagination on his part to realize why it was there, how they intended to kill him. Every nerve in his scalp prickled, as though ants were crawling over his head. He wanted to believe they were bluffing, knew there was no chance. They hadn't gone to all this trouble to simply chastise him and send him on his way like a naughty boy. No way! That steel block hovering ominously was his death sentence and they wanted him to know it, to enjoy him knowing.

One of the men disappeared for a moment, returned with a stool in one hand, a clock in the other. He placed the chair in front of Frank, put the clock on it facing towards him so that he could read the time. It was one o'clock.

'The sands of time are running out for you,' the woman said. 'We haven't a sand dial that could do the job but the clock will do fine.'

All Frank's hopes telescoped to one desire, a quick death. He glared at the woman.

'I loved you once,' he said pathetically. 'So shoot me and get it over with quick.'

The look she gave him could have turned water to stone.

'How did you kill my husband?' she rasped. 'Remind me!'

Frank didn't answer. Whatever he said would be wasted and he knew it.

'Let me remind you, then,' she continued. 'You weren't man enough to face him, so you struck him from behind when he was defenceless, then let your own brother go to gaol.' She laughed like a madwoman. 'All that because I turned you down.'

The boy spoke for the first time. 'He's a worm. My da would have stamped on him.'

The woman patted the boy's head.

'He's going to die the way your da died.'

Frank couldn't help himself. He lifted his eyes upwards to that block of steel. It was hanging there like a giant fist ready to pound him into the concrete, only chains preventing it. Perspiration trickled from every pore in his body, snaked down his spine.

'Yes!' she said. 'Yes! You've got the idea.'

One of the men sniggered and she silenced him with a look, as though, in her mind at least, what she was doing deserved dignity and he had crossed a line.

'But Bull didn't know it was coming,' she said,' and you do, so we'll have to make a little refinement in the name of justice.'

Frank felt exhausted; the tension had drained all his resources. His brain couldn't take any more, started to divorce itself from the proceedings. The figures around him seemed to recede into the distance, the woman's voice to be coming from further away. She saw it happening, wasn't to be denied her satisfaction, struck him twice across the face with the palm of her hand, demanded he look at the clock.

'Sometime within the next twelve hours one of us will return to release those chains,' she said. 'It'll happen dead on the hour but you won't know which one.'

She pushed her face right into his, bored into him with her eyes. They were nothing like the eyes of the innocent young girl he tried to woo all those years ago.

'If I was you,' she continued, straightening up, 'I'd wonder about my Bull waiting to meet you on the other side.'

Frank had had enough, started to shake uncontrollably. In all his life he'd never given more than a passing thought to his own mortality. Now, as though out of nowhere it was at his elbow, a silent desolate creature waiting to rob and defile him. He was very afraid.

'We'll leave you now,' the woman said,' to think about the good man you killed, the son and two daughters you deprived of a father and the widow who still cries at his grave.'

219

He heard them walk away, didn't look up as the echo of their footsteps gradually died. Finally the shaking stopped but he was no better for that; the terror inside remained, an octopus searching out every part of him with its tentacles. A perverse compulsion dragged his eyes to the clock. Only ten minutes had passed. He let out a howl of pain. Now he knew how a trapped animal felt, jaws of steel clamped down on its limbs, a long time to wait before death came to release it from its agony. He lifted his head and howled again, this time so loud it came back at him from the walls like a voice from another world.

He tried his best to wriggle free but it was impossible. The clock gradually became the centre of his existence. Its long, black hands seemed to take on a life of their own, torturing him with unbearable anticipation as they approached each hour, filling him with a sense of relief when it was past and nothing happened. But each relief was short lived, a miniscule respite, because it would start all over again, the hands creeping inexorably forward, dragging him with them to the hour of his doom.

It was five minutes to twelve. His mind was becoming deranged, on the verge of madness. But enough logic survived to know, even if those relentless hands swept past twelve and he was still alive, he'd only have one hour left. He longed for it to be over but if his torturers had let him come this far, surely they'd take him all the way, maximize his suffering.

Only seconds remained of that penultimate hour. Those remorseless hands hovered, teasing his battered brain. His body was as rigid as a corpse with rigor mortis. Nothing existed for him except that clock. He blinked uncontrollably.

The hands struck home. Just for a micro second, he thought the moment had passed. Then the weight of all the world seemed to descend on top of his head and the clock's onward march lost all meaning.

Henry could see Bull Jackson on his knees, a lost look in his eye. A wind was howling, tugging at his hair, rippling the dark field where he kneeled. Behind him stood a shadowy figure in executioner's garb. Henry cried out to warn Bull but he couldn't hear him. Further off, something moved. He saw his father arise from the dark field, eyes wide, mouth open, watching as the executioner struck Bull three mighty blows from behind. Bull fell headlong and the field was transformed into a river of blood. Out of the blood, a face swam up, eyes a lupine yellow, blood dripping from the lips. Frank's lips! Then something dropped from above and the face dissolved to nothing.

He woke with a start, looked at the clock, was surprised it had just turned midday. He lay for a while, pleased that the headache that had plagued him all night had gone away.

Over lunch he told Mary about the dream. She said it wasn't surprising, given how traumatic it must have been for him when he found out what had happened, that it was best not to dwell on it.

'I'm afraid there might be a bit of Frank in me,' he said. 'After all, we're brothers.'

'You're nothing like him,' she said. 'He's cold. The first time I saw him in the pub I knew. You reached out, Henry – to me, to Tom Daly, to John.'

'But sometimes I had no self control. My temper – There

221

was a time I could have kicked off against the whole world.'

'But you didn't. You learned to think twice. You're always telling John to do the same.'

That much was true. He'd struggled with his demons, hoped he'd conquered them. Even at his worst he'd never done anything without provocation, not in cold blood, always in the heat of the moment. Frank had never reached out to anyone except for an ulterior motive, when he stood to profit. He supposed in the end all that really counted was that reaching out, otherwise you were nothing, just a piece of debris floating through an indifferent universe, touching nothing, helping nobody. Like Frank. Cold as stone.